Th.   M000103676

The Popular Girl

F. Scott Fitzgerald

ET REMOTISSIMA PROPE

Modern Voices

Modern Voices
Published by Hesperus Press Limited
4 Rickett Street, London SW6 1RU
www.hesperuspress.com

Designed and typeset by Fraser Muggeridge
Printed in Jordan by Jordan National Press

ISBN: 1-84391-403-4

Contents

Foreword

Our age, with its passion for biography and celebrity, knows more of the psychology of certain writers than it does of their writing. It's far from necessary to read Sylvia Plath or Virginia Woolf, for example, in order to be familiar with versions of their inner lives, sketched in play, film or book. F. Scott Fitzgerald's stories and novels are similarly haunted by what we think we know of the man, before we have read one word. The tabloid story keeps elbowing its way in. Gifted, handsome, oversensitive boy from St Paul, Minnesota, hungry for fame, falls in love with Southern belle, goes from rags to riches when first novel is published to dazzling success, gets the girl and sets New York alight. And after the success, the excess. Jazz Age, Roaring Twenties, parties, Paris, stories sold for three thousand dollars apiece, more and more parties, and then the crash, the slump, and the long slide into debt, alcoholism, sickness and despair. Only the recovery and final flowering of a great talent in *The Last Tycoon* spoils the contour of this artistic morality tale.

But of course it was Fitzgerald, rather than newspapers or biographers, who first and most brilliantly blurred the line between his life and his art. He made the story, wrote it, lived it, and in doing so taxed his body and spirit to their limits. As he observed, 'I have asked a lot of my emotions – one hundred and twenty stories. The price was high, right up with Kipling, because there was a little drop of something – not blood, not a tear, not my seed, but me more intimately than these, in every story...' (*The Crack-Up*, 1945). The way that Fitzgerald held nothing back may seem reckless, but it was part of his very individual code. Fitzgerald admired courage above most virtues. Physical courage, certainly, but most especially those qualities of moral and spiritual courage which accept that calls beyond reason are made on a human being, and must be answered.

The five stories published here are much concerned with the possibility of defeat. Their chief characters are vulnerable, and may not survive. Beautiful young Yanci Bowman is holed up in the Ritz with ten cents to her name, desperate for the only solution her tradition and upbringing leaves open to her. Henry Marston, blackmailed by his wife and her lover, swims against a strong tide towards a lighthouse, with his children's future sealed in a pouch around his neck. Handsome Dick Ragland sets off to meet a lovely girl after a night of heavy drinking, unaware that his handsomeness has melted to a 'chin wobbling like a made-over chin in which the paraffin had run – it was a face that both expressed and inspired disgust.'

In all these stories, Fitzgerald is fascinated by the narrow margin dividing a life that coheres from one that disintegrates. He writes with enormous persuasiveness about flashes of joy, moments of intense, overwhelming vitality, and the tenderness and brilliance of first love, but enduring contentment is not, on the whole, his subject here. As he observed in his memoir *The Crack-Up*: 'This is what I think now: that the natural state of the sentient adult is a qualified unhappiness.' But it is in the way Fitzgerald paints the qualifications that he reveals the depth of his artistry, and the incomparable loveliness of certain moments in life.

In 'A New Leaf' Julia Ross, who will fall so hopelessly in love with alcoholic Dick Ragland, sits in an outdoor cafe in the Bois de Boulogne. It is Spring, the chestnut flowers fall on the tables, and Julia is absurdly happy. Just as she sees Dick for the first time, Fitzgerald quotes three lines from Shelley's 'Stanzas Written in Dejection Near Naples'. We do not quite know if these lines are in Julia's mind, or in the author's. The poem anticipates death by water, and has been seen as a portent of Shelley's drowning. Dick Ragland, too, will vanish in mid-ocean, one among the icons of self-destruction which haunt Fitzgerald's fiction.

Fitzgerald leaves these parallels between the poem and the under-lying movement of his story to develop in the reader's mind, as the first scene unfolds between Dick and Julia. His extraordinary feeling for each story's rhythm allows him to leave such beats, silences, spaces. To read a Fitzgerald story is to enter a state of discovery, rather than one in which information is given.

Shelley, like Keats, was one of Fitzgerald's artistic lodestars. But Fitzgerald is not a 'poetic' prose writer, if that implies, as it often does, an overindulgence in adjectives and adverbs and a tendency towards decorative texture which has no narrative function. Fitzgerald loved the economic sensuousness of poetry as much as he loved its mastery of cadence, and these qualities make his own prose some of the most memorable ever written. He crystallised his receptivity into defining phrases: 'the diamond as big as the Ritz', 'the dark fields of the Republic', 'the green light at the end of Daisy's dock'. At the end of 'The Swimmers', a story which anticipates and echoes *Tender is the Night*, Fitzgerald meditates on the character of his native land. He begins with the thought that while France is a land and England a people, America, 'having about it that quality of the idea, was harder to utter'. He goes on to instance 'the graves at Shiloh, and the tired, drawn, nervous faces of its great men', but he is not finished yet. A classic Fitzgeraldian defining phrase concludes the meditation, and the story. America is 'a willingness of the heart'.

'The Swimmers', 'Love in the Night' and 'The Popular Girl' are fundamentally optimistic in their moral framework. The protagonist of 'Love in the Night', Val Rostoff, a young Russian prince who becomes a post-revolutionary émigré in the South of France, forms a hyper-romantic attachment after one meeting. This is a subtle story about apparently obvious transformations. Prince becomes pauper, unattainable girl becomes lonely widow, Russia's ruling class become taxi drivers. But… the story is not over. Val's inner transformation begins when he discovers in himself the American drive of his mother and grandfather, and that a life of princely privilege has, paradoxically, impoverished him.

'The Popular Girl' treats impoverishment from a different angle. Yanci Bowman, a typical Fitzgerald Southern girl, is lovely, self-willed, and underused. But her hard-drinking father dies penniless, and Yanci, initially outraged, becomes a strategist. She will not accept the condition into which life has thrown her, any more than Val will settle for a life harking back to former glories. 'The Swimmers' is less of a fairy tale. Adultery, mental strain and double-dealing almost ruin Henry Marston. He nearly succumbs to the despair of the virtuous man in a world which seems emptied of virtue. But Henry's situation is recoverable, because he does not feel that he has colluded in his own tragedy.

Henry Marston's story and character resemble those of Dick Diver in *Tender is the Night*, but the themes are less deeply worked, and

Henry Marston is a less remarkable man. However, it is fascinating to note how often a return to American values indicates a character's moral and spiritual replenishment. Incisive as Fitzgerald can be about the American culture of success – his sporting hero and heroine in 'What a Handsome Pair!' are elegantly satirised, and Helen Van Beck is surely sister to *The Great Gatsby*'s ruthless Jordan Baker – ultimately he loves something of what it represents. The sportsman in 'What a Handsome Pair!' is allowed his heroic destiny.

The five stories printed here are polished facets of Fitzgerald's lifelong preoccupations. Some characters dwindle in the face of their experiences, other close down the hatches in the face of pain and refuse to feel any more, but those who interest Fitzgerald most continue to affront their destinies. They do so with that fine, candid courage against all odds, which was perhaps the quality he loved best.

– *Helen Dunmore, 2005*

The Popular Girl

Along about half-past ten every Saturday night Yanci Bowman eluded her partner by some graceful subterfuge and from the dancing floor went to a point of vantage overlooking the country-club bar. When she saw her father she would either beckon to him, if he chanced to be looking in her direction, or else she would dispatch a waiter to call attention to her impendent presence. If it were no later than half-past ten – that is, if he had had no more than an hour of synthetic gin rickeys – he would get up from his chair and suffer himself to be persuaded into the ballroom.

'Ballroom', for want of a better word. It was that room, filled by day with wicker furniture, which was always connotated in the phrase 'Let's go in and dance.' It was referred to as 'inside' or 'downstairs'. It was that nameless chamber wherein occur the principal transactions of all the country clubs in America.

Yanci knew that if she could keep her father there for an hour, talking, watching her dance, or even on rare occasions dancing himself, she could safely release him at the end of that time. In the period that would elapse before midnight ended the dance he could scarcely become sufficiently stimulated to annoy anyone.

All this entailed considerable exertion on Yanci's part, and it was less for her father's sake than for her own that she went through with it. Several rather unpleasant experiences were scattered through this last summer. One night when she had been detained by the impassioned and impossible-to-interrupt speech of a young man from Chicago her father had appeared swaying gently in the ballroom doorway; in his ruddy handsome face two faded blue eyes were squinted half shut as he tried to focus them on the dancers, and he was obviously preparing to offer himself to the first dowager who caught his eye. He was ludicrously injured when Yanci insisted upon an immediate withdrawal.

After that night Yanci went through her Fabian manoeuvre to the minute.

Yanci and her father were the handsomest two people in the Middle Western city where they lived. Tom Bowman's complexion was hearty from twenty years spent in the service of good whiskey and bad golf. He kept an office downtown, where he was thought to transact some vague real-estate business; but in point of fact his chief concern in life was the exhibition of a handsome profile and an easy well-bred manner at the country club, where he had spent the greater part of the ten years that had elapsed since his wife's death.

Yanci was twenty, with a vague die-away manner which was partly the setting for her languid disposition and partly the effect of a visit she had paid to some Eastern relatives at an impressionable age. She was intelligent, in a flitting way, romantic under the moon and unable to decide whether to marry for sentiment or for comfort, the latter of these two abstractions being well enough personified by one of the most ardent among her admirers. Meanwhile she kept house not without efficiency, for her father, and tried in a placid unruffled tempo to regulate his constant tippling to the sober side of inebriety.

She admired her father. She admired him for his fine appearance and for his charming manner. He had never quite lost the air of having been a popular Bonesman at Yale[1]. This charm of his was a standard by which her susceptible temperament unconsciously judged the men she knew. Nevertheless, father and daughter were far from that sentimental family relationship which is a stock plant in fiction, but in life usually exists in the mind of only the older party to it. Yanci Bowman had decided to leave her home by marriage within the year. She was heartily bored.

Scott Kimberly, who saw her for the first time this November evening at the country club, agreed with the lady whose house guest he was that Yanci was an exquisite beauty. With a sort of conscious sensuality surprising in such a young man – Scott was only twenty-five – he avoided an introduction that he might watch her undisturbed for a fanciful hour, and sip the pleasure or the disillusion of her conversation at the drowsy end of the evening.

'She never got over the disappointment of not meeting the Prince of Wales when he was in the country,' remarked Mrs Orrin Rogers, following his gaze. 'She said so, anyhow; whether she was serious or not I don't know. I hear that she has her walls simply plastered with pictures of him.'

'Who?' asked Scott suddenly.

'Why, the Prince of Wales.'

'Who has plaster pictures of him?'

'Why, Yanci Bowman, the girl you said you thought was so pretty.'

'After a certain degree of prettiness, one pretty girl is as pretty as another,' said Scott argumentatively.

'Yes, I suppose so.'

Mrs Rogers' voice drifted off on an indefinite note. She had never in her life compassed a generality until it had fallen familiarly on her ear for constant repetition.

'Let's talk her over,' Scott suggested.

With a mock reproachful smile Mrs Rogers lent herself agreeably to slander. An encore was just beginning. The orchestra trickled a light overflow of music into the pleasant green-latticed room and the two score couples who for the evening comprised the local younger set moved placidly into time with its beat. Only a few apathetic stags gathered one by one in the doorways, and to a close observer it was apparent that the scene did not attain the gaiety which was its aspiration. These girls and men had known each other from childhood; and though there were marriages incipient upon the floor tonight, they were marriages of environment, of resignation, or even of boredom.

Their trappings lacked the sparkle of the seventeen-year-old affairs that took place through the short and radiant holidays. On such occasions as this, thought Scott as his eyes still sought casually for Yanci, occurred the matings of the leftovers, the plainer, the duller, the poorer of the social world; matings actuated by the same urge towards perhaps a more glamorous destiny, yet, for all that, less beautiful and less young. Scott himself was feeling very old.

But there was one face in the crowd to which his generalisation did not apply. When his eyes found Yanci Bowman among the dancers he felt much younger. She was the incarnation of all in which the dance failed – graceful youth, arrogant, languid freshness and beauty that was sad and perishable as a memory in a dream. Her partner, a young man with one of those fresh red complexions ribbed with white streaks, as though he had been slapped on a cold day, did not appear to be holding her interest, and her glance fell here and there upon a group, a face, a garment, with a far-away and oblivious melancholy.

'Dark blue eyes,' said Scott to Mrs Rogers. 'I don't know that they mean anything except that they're beautiful, but that nose and upper lip and chin are certainly aristocratic – if there is any such thing,' he added apologetically.

'Oh, she's very aristocratic,' agreed Mrs Rogers. 'Her grandfather was a senator or governor or something in one of the Southern States. Her father's very aristocratic-looking too. Oh, yes, they're very aristocratic; they're aristocratic people.'

'She looks lazy.'

Scott was watching the yellow gown drift and submerge among the dancers.

'She doesn't like to move. It's a wonder she dances so well. Is she engaged? Who is the man who keeps cutting in on her, the one who tucks his tie under his collar so rakishly and affects the remarkable slanting pockets?'

He was annoyed at the young man's persistence, and his sarcasm lacked the ring of detachment.

'Oh, that's' – Mrs Rogers bent forwards, the tip of her tongue just visible between her lips – 'that's the O'Rourke boy. He's quite devoted, I believe.'

'I believe,' Scott said suddenly, 'that I'll get you to introduce me if she's near when the music stops.'

They arose and stood looking for Yanci – Mrs Rogers, small, stoutening, nervous, and Scott Kimberly her husband's cousin, dark and just below medium height. Scott was an orphan with half a million of his own, and he was in this city for no more reason than that he had missed a train. They looked for several minutes, and in vain. Yanci, in her yellow dress, no longer moved with slow loveliness among the dancers.

The clock stood at half-past ten.

2

'Good evening,' her father was saying to her at that moment in syllables faintly slurred. 'This seems to be getting to be a habit.'

They were standing near a side stairs, and over his shoulder through a glass door Yanci could see a party of half a dozen men sitting in familiar joviality about a round table.

'Don't you want to come out and watch for a while?' she suggested, smiling and affecting a casualness she did not feel.

'Not tonight, thanks.'

Her father's dignity was a bit too emphasised to be convincing.

'Just come out and take a look,' she urged him. 'Everybody's here and I want to ask you what you think of somebody.'

This was not so good, but it was the best that occurred to her.

'I doubt very strongly if I'd find anything to interest me out there,' said Tom Bowman emphatically. 'I observe that f'some insane reason I'm always taken out and aged on the wood for half an hour as though I was irresponsible.'

'I only ask you to stay a little while.'

'Very considerate, I'm sure. But tonight I happ'n be interested in a discussion that's taking place in here.'

'Come on, Father.'

Yanci put her arm through his ingratiatingly, but he released it by the simple expedient of raising his own arm and letting hers drop.

'I'm afraid not.'

'I'll tell you,' she suggested lightly, concealing her annoyance at this unusually protracted argument, 'you come in and look, just once, and then if it bores you you can go right back.'

He shook his head.

'No thanks.'

Then without another word he turned suddenly and re-entered the bar. Yanci went back to the ballroom. She glanced easily at the stag line as she passed, and making a quick selection murmured to a man near her, 'Dance with me, will you, Carty? I've lost my partner.'

'Glad to,' answered Carty truthfully.

'Awfully sweet of you.'

'Sweet of me? Of you, you mean.'

She looked up at him absently. She was furiously annoyed at her father. Next morning at breakfast she would radiate a consuming chill, but for tonight she could only wait, hoping that if the worst happened he would at least remain in the bar until the dance was over.

Mrs Rogers, who lived next door to the Bowmans, appeared suddenly at her elbow with a strange young man.

'Yanci,' Mrs Rogers was saying with a social smile. 'I want to introduce Mr Kimberly. Mr Kimberly's spending the weekend with us, and I particularly wanted him to meet you.'

'How perfectly slick!' drawled Yanci with lazy formality.

Mr Kimberly suggested to Miss Bowman that they dance, to which proposal Miss Bowman dispassionately acquiesced. They mingled their arms in the gesture prevalent and stepped into time with the beat of the drum. Simultaneously it seemed to Scott that the room and the couples who danced up and down upon it converted themselves into a background behind her. The commonplace lamps, the rhythm of the music playing some paraphrase of a paraphrase, the faces of many girls, pretty, undistinguished or absurd, assumed a certain solidity as though they grouped themselves into a retinue for Yanci's languid eyes and dancing feet.

'I've been watching you,' said Scott simply. 'You look rather bored this evening.'

'Do I?' Her dark blue eyes exposed a borderland of fragile iris as they opened in a delicate burlesque of interest. 'How perfectly kill-ing!' she added.

Scott laughed. She had used the exaggerated phrase without smiling, indeed without any attempt to give it verisimilitude. He had heard the adjectives of the year – 'hectic', 'marvellous' and 'slick' – delivered casually, but never before without the faintest meaning. In this lackadaisical young beauty it was inexpressibly charming.

The dance ended. Yanci and Scott strolled towards a lounge set against the wall, but before they could take possession there was a shriek of laughter and a brawny damsel dragging an embarrassed boy in her wake skidded by them and plumped down upon it.

'How rude!' observed Yanci.

'I suppose it's her privilege.'

'A girl with ankles like that has no privileges.'

They seated themselves uncomfortably on two stiff chairs.

'Where do you come from?' she asked Scott with polite disinterest.

'New York.'

This having transpired, Yanci deigned to fix her eyes on him for the best part of ten seconds.

'Who was the gentleman with the invisible tie,' Scott asked rudely, in order to make her look at him again, 'who was giving you such a rush? I found it impossible to keep my eyes off him. Is his personality as diverting as his haberdashery?'

'I don't know,' she drawled; 'I've only been engaged to him for a week.'

'My Lord!' exclaimed Scott, perspiring suddenly under his eyes. 'I beg your pardon. I didn't –'

'I was only joking,' she interrupted with a sighing laugh. 'I thought I'd see what you'd say to that.'

Then they both laughed, and Yanci continued, 'I'm still not engaged to anyone. I'm too horribly unpopular.' Still the same key, her languorous voice humorously contradicting the content of her remark. 'No one'll ever marry me.'

'How pathetic!'

'Really,' she murmured; 'because I have to have compliments all the time, in order to live, and no one thinks I'm attractive any more, so no one ever gives them to me.'

Seldom had Scott been so amused.

'Why, you beautiful child,' he cried, 'I'll bet you never hear anything else from morning till night!'

'Oh, yes I do,' she responded, obviously pleased. 'I never get compliments unless I fish for them.'

'Everything's the same,' she was thinking as she gazed around her in a peculiar mood of pessimism. Same boys sober and same boys tight; same old women sitting by the walls – and one or two girls sitting with them who were dancing this time last year.

Yanci had reached the stage where these country-club dances seemed little more than a display of sheer idiocy. From being an enchanted carnival where jewelled and immaculate maidens rouged to the pinkest propriety displayed themselves to strange and fascinating men, the picture had faded to a medium-sized hall where was an almost indecent display of unclothed motives and obvious failures. So much for several years! And the dance had changed scarcely by a ruffle in the fashions or a new flip in a figure of speech.

Yanci was ready to be married.

Meanwhile the dozen remarks rushing to Scott Kimberly's lips were interrupted by the apologetic appearance of Mrs Rogers.

'Yanci,' the older woman was saying, 'the chauffeur's just telephoned to say that the car's broken down. I wonder if you and your father have room for us going home. If it's the slightest inconvenience don't hesitate to tell –'

'I know he'll be terribly glad to. He's got loads of room, because I came out with someone else.'

She was wondering if her father would be presentable at twelve.

He could always drive at any rate – and, besides, people who asked for a lift could take what they got.

'That'll be lovely. Thank you so much,' said Mrs Rogers.

Then, as she had just passed the kittenish late thirties when women still think they are *persona grata* with the young and entered upon the early forties when their children convey to them tactfully that they no longer are, Mrs Rogers obliterated herself from the scene. At that moment the music started and the unfortunate young man with white streaks in his red complexion appeared in front of Yanci.

Just before the end of the next dance Scott Kimberly cut in on her again.

'I've come back,' he began, 'to tell you how beautiful you are.'

'I'm not, really,' she answered. 'And besides, you tell everyone that.'

The music gathered gusto for its finale, and they sat down upon the comfortable lounge.

'I've told no one that for three years,' said Scott.

There was no reason why he should have made it three years, yet somehow it sounded convincing to both of them. Her curiosity was stirred. She began finding out about him. She put him to a lazy questionnaire which began with his relationship to the Rogerses and ended, he knew not by what steps, with a detailed description of his apartment in New York.

'I want to live in New York,' she told him; 'on Park Avenue, in one of those beautiful white buildings that have twelve big rooms in each apartment and cost a fortune to rent.'

'That's what I'd want, too, if I were married. Park Avenue – it's one of the most beautiful streets in the world, I think, perhaps chiefly because it hasn't any leprous park trying to give it an artificial sub-urbanity.'

'Whatever that is,' agreed Yanci. 'Anyway, Father and I go to New York about three times a year. We always go to the Ritz.'

This was not precisely true. Once a year she generally pried her father from his placid and not unbeneficent existence that she might spend a week lolling by the Fifth Avenue shop windows, lunching or having tea with some former school friend from Farmover, and occasionally going to dinner and the theatre with the boys who came up from Yale or Princeton for the occasion. These had been pleasant adventures – not one but was filled to the brim with colourful hours – dancing at Mont Martre, dining at the Ritz, with some movie star or supereminent society woman at the next table, or else dreaming of what she might buy at Hempel's or Waxe's or Thrumble's if her father's income had but one additional nought on the happy side of the decimal. She adored New York with a great impersonal affection – adored it as only a Middle-western or Southern girl can. In its gaudy bazaars she felt her soul transported with turbulent delight, for to her eyes it held nothing ugly, nothing sordid, nothing plain.

She had stayed once at the Ritz – once only. The Manhattan, where they usually registered, had been torn down. She knew that she could never induce her father to afford the Ritz again.

After a moment she borrowed a pencil and paper and scribbled a notification 'To Mr Bowman in the grill' that he was expected to drive Mrs Rogers and her guest home, 'by request' – this last underlined. She hoped that he would be able to do so with dignity. This note she sent by a waiter to her father. Before the next dance began it was returned to her with a scrawled OK and her father's initials.

The remainder of the evening passed quickly. Scott Kimberly cut

11

in on her as often as time permitted, giving her those comforting assurances of her enduring beauty which, not without a whimsical pathos, she craved. He laughed at her also, and she was not sure that she liked that. In common with all vague people, she was unaware that she was vague. She did not entirely comprehend when Scott Kimberly told her that her personality would endure long after she was too old to care whether it endured or not.

She liked best to talk about New York, and each of their interrupted conversations gave her a picture or a memory of the metropolis on which she speculated as she looked over the shoulder of Jerry O'Rourke or Carty Braden or some other beau, to whom, as to all of them, she was comfortable anaesthetic. At midnight she sent another note to her father, saying that Mrs Rogers and Mrs Rogers' guest would meet him immediately on the porch by the driveway. Then, hoping for the best, she walked out into the starry night and was assisted by Jerry O'Rourke into his roadster.

3

'Goodnight, Yanci.' With her late escort she was standing on the kerbstone in front of the rented stucco house where she lived. Mr O'Rourke was attempting to put significance into his lingering rendition of her name. For weeks he had been straining to boost their relations almost forcibly onto a sentimental plane, but Yanci, with her vague impassivity, which was a defence against almost anything, had brought to naught his efforts. Jerry O'Rourke was an old story. His family had money, but he – he worked in a brokerage house along with most of the rest of his young generation. He sold bonds – bonds were the new thing; real estate was once the thing – in the days of the boom; then automobiles were the thing. Bonds were the thing now. Young men sold them who had nothing else to go into.

'Don't bother to come up, please.' Then as he put his car into gear, 'Call me up soon!'

A minute later he turned the corner of the moonlit street and disappeared, his cut-out resounding voluminously through the night as it declared that the rest of two dozen weary inhabitants was of no concern to his gay meanderings.

Yanci sat down thoughtfully upon the porch steps. She had no key and must wait for her father's arrival. Five minutes later a roadster turned into the street, and approaching with exaggerated caution stopped in front of the Rogers' large house next door. Relieved, Yanci arose and strolled slowly down the walk. The door of the car had swung open and Mrs Rogers, assisted by Scott Kimberly, had alighted safely upon the sidewalk; but to Yanci's surprise Scott Kimberly, after escorting Mrs Rogers to her steps, returned to the car. Yanci was close enough to notice that he took the driver's seat. As he drew up at the Bowmans' kerbstone Yanci saw that her father was occupying the far corner, fighting with ludicrous dignity against a sleep that had come upon him. She groaned. The fatal last hour had done its work – Tom Bowman was once more *hors de combat*.

'Hello,' cried Yanci as she reached the kerb.

'Yanci,' muttered her parent, simulating, unsuccessfully, a brisk welcome. His lips were curved in an ingratiating grin.

'Your father wasn't feeling quite fit, so he let me drive home,' explained Scott cheerfully as he got himself out and came up to her.

'Nice little car. Had it long?'

Yanci laughed, but without humour.

'Is he paralysed?'

'Is who paralyse'?' demanded the figure in the car with an offended sigh.

Scott was standing by the car.

'Can I help you out, sir?'

'I c'n get out. I c'n get out,' insisted Mr Bowman. 'Just step a li'l out my way. Someone must have given me some stremely bad wisk'.'

'You mean a lot of people must have given you some,' retorted Yanci in cold unsympathy.

Mr Bowman reached the kerb with astonishing ease, but this was a deceitful success, for almost immediately he clutched at a handle of air perceptible only to himself, and was saved by Scott's quickly proffered arm. Followed by the two men, Yanci walked towards the house in a furore of embarrassment. Would the young man think that such scenes went on every night? It was chiefly her own presence that made it humiliating for Yanci. Had her father been carried to bed by two butlers each evening she might even have been proud of the fact that he could afford such dissipation; but to have it thought that she assisted, that she was burdened with the worry and the care! And finally she was annoyed with Scott Kimberly for being there, and for his officiousness in helping her father into the house.

Reaching the low porch of tapestry brick, Yanci searched in Tom Bowman's vest for the key and unlocked the front door. A minute later the master of the house was deposited in an easy chair.

'Thanks very much,' he said, recovering for a moment. 'Sit down. Like a drink? Yanci, get some crackers and cheese, if there's any, won't you, dear?'

At the unconscious coolness of this Scott and Yanci laughed.

'It's your bedtime, Father,' she said, her anger struggling with diplomacy.

'Give me my guitar,' he suggested, 'and I'll play you tune.'

Except on such occasions as this, he had not touched his guitar for twenty years. Yanci turned to Scott.

'He'll be fine now. Thanks a lot. He'll fall asleep in a minute and when I wake him he'll go to bed like a lamb.'

'Well –'

They strolled together out the door.

'Sleepy?' he asked.

'No, not a bit.'

'Then perhaps you'd better let me stay here with you a few minutes until you see if he's all right. Mrs Rogers gave me a key so I can get in without disturbing her.'

'It's quite all right,' protested Yanci. 'I don't mind a bit, and he won't be any trouble. He must have taken a glass too much, and this whisky we have out here – you know! This has happened once before – last year,' she added.

Her words satisfied her; as an explanation it seemed to have a convincing ring.

'Can I sit down for a moment, anyway?' They sat side by side upon a wicker porch settee.

'I'm thinking of staying over a few days,' Scott said.

'How lovely!' Her voice had resumed its die-away note.

'Cousin Pete Rogers wasn't well today, but tomorrow he's going duck-shooting, and he wants me to go with him.'

'Oh, how thrill-ing! I've always been mad to go, and Father's always promised to take me, but he never has.'

'We're going to be gone about three days, and then I thought I'd come back here and stay over the next weekend –' He broke off suddenly and bent forward in a listening attitude.

'Now what on earth is that?'

The sounds of music were proceeding brokenly from the room they had lately left – a ragged chord on a guitar and half a dozen feeble starts.

'It's Father!' cried Yanci.

And now a voice drifted out to them, drunken and murmurous, taking the long notes with attempted melancholy:

Sing a song of cities,
Ridin' on a rail,
A niggah's ne'er so happy
As when he's out-a-jail.

'How terrible!' exclaimed Yanci. 'He'll wake everybody in the block.'

The chorus ended, the guitar jangled again, then gave out a last harsh 'spang!' and was still. A moment later these disturbances were followed by a low but quite definite snore. Mr Bowman, having indulged his musical proclivity, had dropped off to sleep.

'Let's go to ride,' suggested Yanci impatiently. 'This is too hectic for me.'

Scott rose with alacrity and they walked down to the car.

'Where'll we go?' she wondered.

'I don't care.'

'We might go up half a block to Crest Avenue – that's our show street – and then ride out to the river boulevard.'

4

As they turned into Crest Avenue the new cathedral, immense and unfinished, in imitation of a cathedral left unfinished by accident in some little Flemish town, squatted just across the way like a plump white bulldog on its haunches. The ghosts of four moonlit apostles looked down at them wanly from wall niches still littered with the white dusty trash of the builders. The cathedral inaugurated Crest Avenue. After it came the great brownstone mass built by R.R. Comerford, the flour king, followed by a half mile of pretentious stone houses put up in the gloomy '90s. These were adorned with monstrous driveways and porte cochères which had once echoed to the hooves of good horses and with huge circular windows that corseted the second storeys.

The continuity of these mausoleums was broken by a small park, a triangle of grass where Nathan Hale[2] stood ten feet tall with his hands bound behind his back by stone cord and stared over a great bluff at the slow Mississippi. Crest Avenue ran along the bluff, but neither faced it nor seemed aware of it, for all the houses fronted inward towards the street. Beyond the first half mile it became newer, essayed ventures in terraced lawns, in concoctions of stucco or in granite mansions which imitated through a variety of gradual refinements the marble contours of the Petit Trianon. The houses of this phase rushed by the roadster for a succession of minutes; then the way turned and the car was headed directly into the moonlight which swept towards it like the lamp of some gigantic motorcycle far up the avenue.

Past the low Corinthian lines of the Christian Science Temple, past a block of dark frame horrors, a deserted row of grim red brick – an unfortunate experiment of the late '90s – then new houses again, bright red brick now, with trimmings of white, black iron fences and hedges binding flowery lawns. These swept by, faded, passed, enjoying their moment of grandeur; then waiting there in the moonlight to be outmoded as had the frame, cupolaed mansions of lower town and the brownstone piles of older Crest Avenue in their turn.

The roofs lowered suddenly, the lots narrowed, the houses shrank up in size and shaded off into bungalows. These held the street for the last mile, to the bend in the river which terminated the prideful avenue at the statue of Chelsea Arbuthnot. Arbuthnot was the first governor – and almost the last of Anglo-Saxon blood.

All the way thus far Yanci had not spoken, absorbed still in the annoyance of the evening, yet soothed somehow by the fresh air of northern November that rushed by them. She must take her fur coat out of storage next day, she thought.

'Where are we now?'

As they slowed down Scott looked up curiously at the pompous stone figure, clear in the crisp moonlight, with one hand on a book and the forefinger of the other pointing, as though with reproachful symbolism, directly at some construction work going on in the street.

'This is the end of Crest Avenue,' said Yanci, turning to him. 'This is our show street.'

'A museum of American architectural failures.'

'What?'

'Nothing,' he murmured.

'I should have explained it to you. I forgot. We can go along the river boulevard if you'd like – or are you tired?'

Scott assured her that he was not tired – not in the least.

Entering the boulevard, the cement road twisted under darkling trees.

'The Mississippi – how little it means to you now!' said Scott suddenly.

'What?' Yanci looked around. 'Oh, the river.'

'I guess it was once pretty important to your ancestors up here.'

'My ancestors weren't up here then,' said Yanci with some dignity. 'My ancestors were from Maryland. My father came out here when he left Yale.'

'Oh!' Scott was politely impressed.

'My mother was from here. My father came out here from Baltimore because of his health.'

'Oh!'

'Of course we belong here now, I suppose' – this with faint condescension – 'as much as anywhere else.'

'Of course.'

'Except that I want to live in the East and I can't persuade Father to,' she finished.

It was after one o'clock and the boulevard was almost deserted. Occasionally two yellow disks would top a rise ahead of them and take shape as a late-returning automobile. Except for that they were alone in a continual rushing dark. The moon had gone down.

'Next time the road goes near the river let's stop and watch it,' he suggested.

Yanci smiled inwardly. This remark was obviously what one boy of her acquaintance had named an international petting cue, by which was meant a suggestion that aimed to create naturally a situation for a kiss. She considered the matter. As yet the man had made no particular impression on her. He was good-looking, apparently well-to-do and from New York. She had begun to like him during the dance, increasingly as the evening had drawn to a close; then the incident of her father's appalling arrival had thrown cold water upon this tentative warmth; and now – it was November, and the night was cold. Still –

'All right,' she agreed suddenly.

The road divided; she swerved around and brought the car to a stop in an open place high above the river.

'Well?' she demanded in the deep quiet that followed the shutting off of the engine.

'Thanks.'

'Are you satisfied here?'

'Almost. Not quite.'

'Why not?'

'I'll tell you in a minute,' he answered. 'Why is your name Yanci?'

'It's a family name.'

'It's very pretty.' He repeated it several times caressingly. 'Yanci – it has all the grace of Nancy, and yet it isn't prim.'

'What's your name?' she enquired.

'Scott.'

'Scott what?'

'Kimberly. Did you know?'

'I wasn't sure. Mrs Rogers introduced you in such a mumble.'

There was a slight pause.

'Yanci,' he repeated; 'beautiful Yanci, with her dark blue eyes and her lazy soul. Do you know why I'm not quite satisfied, Yanci?'

'Why?'

Imperceptibly she had moved her face nearer until as she waited for an answer with her lips faintly apart he knew that in asking she had granted.

Without haste he bent his head forward and touched her lips.

He sighed, and both of them felt a sort of relief – relief from the embarrassment of playing up to what conventions of this sort of thing remained.

'Thanks,' he said as he had when she first stopped the car.

'Now are you satisfied?'

Her blue eyes regarded him unsmilingly in the darkness.

'After a fashion; of course, you can never say – definitely.'

Again he bent towards her, but she stooped and started the motor. It was late and Yanci was beginning to be tired. What purpose there was in the experiment was accomplished. He had had what he asked. If he liked it he would want more, and that put her one move ahead in the game which she felt she was beginning.

'I'm hungry,' she complained. 'Let's go down and eat.'

'Very well,' he acquiesced sadly. 'Just when I was so enjoying – the Mississippi.'

'Do you think I'm beautiful?' she enquired almost plaintively as they backed out.

'What an absurd question!'

'But I like to hear people say so.'

'I was just about to – when you started the engine.'

Downtown in a deserted all-night lunch room they ate bacon and eggs. She was pale as ivory now. The night had drawn the lazy vitality and languid colour out of her face. She encouraged him to talk to her of New York until he was beginning every sentence with, 'Well, now, let's see –'

The repast over, they drove home. Scott helped her put the car in the little garage, and just outside the front door she lent him her lips again for the faint brush of a kiss. Then she went in.

The long living room which ran the width of the small stucco house was reddened by a dying fire which had been high when Yanci left and now was faded to a steady undancing glow. She took a log from the firebox and threw it on the embers, then started as a voice came out of the half darkness at the other end of the room.

'Back so soon?'

It was her father's voice, not yet sober, but alert and intelligent.

'Yes. Went riding,' she answered shortly, sitting down in a wicker chair before the fire. 'Then went down and had something to eat.'

'Oh!'

Her father left his place and moved to a chair nearer the fire, where he stretched himself out with a sigh. Glancing at him from the corner of her eye, for she was going to show an appropriate coldness, Yanci was fascinated by his complete recovery of dignity in the space of two hours. His greying hair was scarcely rumpled; his handsome face was ruddy as ever. Only his eyes, criss-crossed with tiny red lines, were evidence of his late dissipation.

'Have a good time?'

'Why should you care?' she answered rudely.

'Why shouldn't I?'

'You didn't seem to care earlier in the evening. I asked you to take two people home for me, and you weren't able to drive your own car.'

'The deuce I wasn't!' he protested. 'I could have driven in – in a race in an arana, areaena. That Mrs Rogers insisted that her young admirer should drive, so what could I do?'

'That isn't her young admirer,' retorted Yanci crisply. There was no drawl in her voice now. 'She's as old as you are. That's her niece – I mean her nephew.'

'Excuse me!'

'I think you owe me an apology.' She found suddenly that she bore him no resentment. She was rather sorry for him and it occurred to her that in asking him to take Mrs Rogers home she had somehow imposed on his liberty. Nevertheless, discipline was necessary – there would be other Saturday nights. 'Don't you?' she concluded.

'I apologise, Yanci.'

'Very well, I accept your apology,' she answered stiffly.

'What's more, I'll make it up to you.'

Her blue eyes contracted. She hoped – she hardly dared to hope that he might take her to New York.

'Let's see,' he said. 'November, isn't it? What date?'

'The twenty-third.'

'Well, I'll tell you what I'll do.' He knocked the tips of his fingers together tentatively. 'I'll give you a present. I've been meaning to let you have a trip all fall, but business has been bad.' She almost smiled – as though business was of any consequence in his life. 'But then you need a trip. I'll make you a present of it.'

He rose again, and crossing over to his desk sat down.

'I've got a little money in a New York bank that's been lying there quite a while,' he said as he fumbled in a drawer for a cheque book. 'I've been intending to close out the account. Let – me – see. There's just –' His pen scratched. 'Where the devil's the blotter? Uh!'

He came back to the fire and a pink oblong paper fluttered into her lap.

'Why, Father!'

It was a cheque for three hundred dollars.

'But can you afford this?' she demanded.

'It's all right,' he reassured her, nodding. 'That can be a Christmas present, too, and you'll probably need a dress or a hat or something before you go.'

'Why,' she began uncertainly, 'I hardly know whether I ought to take this much or not! I've got two hundred of my own downtown, you know. Are you sure –'

'Oh, yes!' He waved his hand with magnificent carelessness. 'You need a holiday. You've been talking about New York, and I want you to go down there. Tell some of your friends at Yale and the other colleges and they'll ask you to the prom or something. That'll be nice. You'll have a good time.'

He sat down abruptly in his chair and gave vent to a long sigh. Yanci folded up the cheque and tucked it into the low bosom of her dress.

'Well,' she drawled softly with a return to her usual manner, 'you're a perfect lamb to be so sweet about it, but I don't want to be horribly extravagant.'

Her father did not answer. He gave her another little sigh and relaxed sleepily into his chair.

'Of course I do want to go,' went on Yanci.

Still her father was silent. She wondered if he were asleep.

'Are you asleep?' she demanded, cheerfully now. She bent towards him; then she stood up and looked at him.

'Father,' she said uncertainly.

Her father remained motionless; the ruddy colour had melted suddenly out of his face.

'Father!'

It occurred to her – and at the thought she grew cold, and a brassiere of iron clutched at her breast – that she was alone in the room. After a frantic instant she said to herself that her father was dead.

5

Yanci judged herself with inevitable gentleness – judged herself very much as a mother might judge a wild, spoilt child. She was not hard-minded, nor did she live by any ordered and considered philosophy of her own. To such a catastrophe as the death of her father her immediate reaction was a hysterical self-pity. The first three days were something of a nightmare, but sentimental civilisation, being as infallible as Nature in healing the wounds of its more fortunate children, had inspired a certain Mrs Oral, whom Yanci had always loathed, with a passionate interest in all such cries. To all intents and purposes Mrs Oral buried Tom Bowman. The morning after his death Yanci had wired her maternal aunt in Chicago, but as yet that undemonstrative and well-to-do lady had sent no answer.

All day long, for four days, Yanci sat in her room upstairs hearing steps come and go on the porch, and it merely increased her nervousness that the doorbell had been disconnected. This by order of Mrs Oral! Doorbells were always disconnected! After the burial of the dead the strain relaxed. Yanci, dressed in her new black, regarded herself in the pier glass, and then wept because she seemed to herself very sad and beautiful. She went downstairs and tried to read a moving-picture magazine, hoping that she would not be alone in the house when the winter dark came down just after four.

This afternoon Mrs Oral had said *carpe diem* to the maid and Yanci was just starting for the kitchen to see whether she had yet gone when the reconnected bell rang suddenly through the house. Yanci started. She waited a minute, then went to the door. It was Scott Kimberly.

'I was just going to enquire for you,' he said.

'Oh! I'm much better, thank you,' she responded with the quiet dignity that seemed suited to her role.

They stood there in the hall awkwardly, each reconstructing the half-facetious, half-sentimental occasion on which they had last met. It seemed such an irreverent prelude to such a sombre disaster. There was no common ground for them now, no gap that could be bridged by a slight reference to their mutual past, and there was no foundation on which he could adequately pretend to share her sorrow.

'Won't you come in?' she said, biting her lip nervously. He followed her to the sitting room and sat beside her on the lounge. In another minute, simply because he was there and alive and friendly, she was crying on his shoulder.

'There, there!' he said, putting his arm behind her and patting her shoulder idiotically. 'There, there, there!'

He was wise enough to attribute no ulterior significance to her action. She was overstrained with grief and loneliness and sentiment; almost any shoulder would have done as well. For all the biological thrill to either of them he might have been a hundred years old. In a minute she sat up.

'I beg your pardon,' she murmured brokenly. 'But it's – it's so dismal in this house today.'

'I know just how you feel, Yanci.'

'Did I – did I – get – tears on your coat?'

In tribute to the tenseness of the incident they both laughed hysterically, and with the laughter she momentarily recovered her propriety.

'I don't know why I should have chosen you to collapse on,' she wailed. 'I really don't just go round doing it indiscriminately on anyone who comes in.'

'I consider it a – a compliment,' he responded soberly, 'and I can understand the state you're in.' Then, after a pause, 'Have you any plans?'

She shook her head.

'Va-vague ones,' she muttered between little gasps. 'I tho-ought I'd go down and stay with my aunt in Chicago a while.'

'I should think that'd be best – much the best thing.' Then, because he could think of nothing else to say, he added, 'Yes, very much the best thing.'

'What are you doing – here in town?' she enquired, taking in her breath in minute gasps and dabbing at her eyes with a handkerchief.

'Oh, I'm here with – with the Rogerses. I've been here.'

'Hunting?'

'No, I've just been here.'

He didn't tell her that he had stayed on her account. She might think it fresh.

'I see,' she said. She didn't see.

'I want to know if there's any possible thing I can do for you, Yanci. Perhaps go downtown for you, or do some errands – anything. Maybe you'd like to bundle up and get a bit of air. I could take you out to drive in your car some night, and no one would see you.'

He clipped his last word short as the inadvertency of this suggestion dawned on him. They stared at each other with horror in their eyes.

'Oh, no, thank you!' she cried. 'I really don't want to drive.'

To his relief the outer door opened and an elderly lady came in. It was Mrs Oral. Scott rose immediately and moved backward towards the door.

'If you're sure there isn't anything I can do –'

Yanci introduced him to Mrs Oral; then leaving the elder woman by the fire walked with him to the door. An idea had suddenly occurred to her.

'Wait a minute.'

She ran up the front stairs and returned immediately with a slip of pink paper in her hand.

'Here's something I wish you'd do,' she said. 'Take this to the First National Bank and have it cashed for me. You can leave the money here for me any time.'

Scott took out his wallet and opened it.

'Suppose I cash it for you now,' he suggested.

'Oh, there's no hurry.'

'But I may as well.' He drew three new one-hundred-dollar bills and gave them to her.

'That's awfully sweet of you,' said Yanci.

'Not at all. May I come in and see you next time I come West?'

'I wish you would.'

'Then I will. I'm going East tonight.'

The door shut him out into the snowy dusk and Yanci returned to Mrs Oral. Mrs Oral had come to discuss plans.

'And now, my dear, just what do you plan to do? We ought to have some plan to go by, and I thought I'd find out if you had any definite plan in your mind.'

Yanci tried to think. She seemed to herself to be horribly alone in the world.

'I haven't heard from my aunt. I wired her again this morning. She may be in Florida.'

'In that case you'd go there?'

'I suppose so.'

'Would you close this house?'

'I suppose so.'

Mrs Oral glanced around with placid practicality. It occurred to her that if Yanci gave the house up she might like it for herself.

'And now,' she continued, 'do you know where you stand financially?'

'All right, I guess,' answered Yanci indifferently; and then with a rush of sentiment, 'There was enough for t-two; there ought to be enough for o-one.'

'I didn't mean that,' said Mrs Oral. 'I mean, do you know the details?'

'No.'

'Well, I thought you didn't know the details. And I thought you ought to know all the details – have a detailed account of what and where your money is. So I called up Mr Haedge, who knew your father very well personally, to come up this afternoon and glance through his papers. He was going to stop in your father's bank, too, by the way, and get all the details there. I don't believe your father left any will.'

Details! Details! Details!

'Thank you,' said Yanci. 'That'll be – nice.'

Mrs Oral gave three or four vigorous nods that were like heavy periods. Then she got up.

'And now if Hilma's gone out I'll make you some tea. Would you like some tea?'

'Sort of.'

'All right, I'll make you some ni-ice tea.'

Tea! Tea! Tea!

Mr Haedge, who came from one of the best Swedish families in town, arrived to see Yanci at five o'clock. He greeted her funereally, said that he had been several times to enquire for her, had organised the pall-bearers and would now find out how she stood in no time. Did she have any idea whether or not there was a will? No? Well, there probably wasn't one.

There was one. He found it almost at once in Mr Bowman's desk – but he worked there until eleven o'clock that night before he found much else. Next morning he arrived at eight, went down to the bank at ten, then to a certain brokerage firm, and came back to Yanci's house at noon. He had known Tom Bowman for some years, but he was utterly astounded when he discovered the condition in which that handsome gallant had left his affairs.

He consulted Mrs Oral, and that afternoon he informed a frightened Yanci in measured language that she was practically penniless. In the midst of the conversation a telegram from Chicago told her that her aunt had sailed the week previous for a trip through the Orient and was not expected back until late spring.

The beautiful Yanci, so profuse, so debonair, so careless with her gorgeous adjectives, had no adjectives for this calamity. She crept upstairs like a hurt child and sat before a mirror, brushing her luxurious hair to comfort herself. One hundred and fifty strokes she gave it, as it said in the treatment, and then a hundred and fifty more – she was too distraught to stop the nervous motion. She brushed it until her arm ached, then she changed arms and went on brushing.

The maid found her next morning, asleep, sprawled across the toilet things on the dresser in a room that was heavy and sweet with the scent of spilt perfume.

6

To be precise, as Mr Haedge was to a depressing degree, Tom Bowman left a bank balance that was more than ample – that is to say, more than ample to supply the post-mortem requirements of his own person. There was also twenty years' worth of furniture, a temperamental roadster with asthmatic cylinders and two one-thousand-dollar bonds of a chain of jewellery stores which yielded seven-and-a-half per cent interest. Unfortunately these were not known in the bond market.

When the car and the furniture had been sold and the stucco bunga-low sublet, Yanci contemplated her resources with dismay. She had a bank balance of almost a thousand dollars. If she invested this she would increase her total income to about fifteen dollars a month. This, as Mrs Oral cheerfully observed, would pay for the boarding-house room she had taken for Yanci as long as Yanci lived. Yanci was so encouraged by this news that she burst into tears.

So she acted as any beautiful girl would have acted in this emergency. With rare decision she told Mr Haedge that she would leave her thousand dollars in a chequing account, and then she walked out of his office and across the street to a beauty parlour to have her hair waved. This raised her morale astonishingly. Indeed, she moved that very day out of the boarding house and into a small room at the best hotel in town. If she must sink into poverty she would at least do so in the grand manner.

Sewed into the lining of her best mourning hat were the three new one-hundred-dollar bills, her father's last present. What she expected of them, why she kept them in such a way, she did not know, unless perhaps because they had come to her under cheerful auspices and might through some gaiety inherent in their crisp and virgin paper buy happier things than solitary meals and narrow hotel beds. They were hope and youth and luck and beauty; they began, somehow, to stand for all the things she had lost in that November night when Tom Bowman, having led her recklessly into space, had plunged off himself, leaving her to find the way back alone.

Yanci remained at the Hiawatha Hotel for three months, and she found that after the first visits of condolence her friends had happier

27

things to do with their time than to spend it in her company. Jerry O'Rourke came to see her one day with a wild Celtic look in his eyes, and demanded that she marry him immediately. When she asked for time to consider he walked out in a rage. She heard later that he had been offered a position in Chicago and had left the same night.

She considered, frightened and uncertain. She had heard of people sinking out of place, out of life. Her father had once told her of a man in his class at college who had become a worker around saloons, polishing brass rails for the price of a can of beer; and she knew also that there were girls in this city with whose mothers her own mother had played as a little girl, but who were poor now and had grown common, who worked in stores and had married into the proletariat. But that such a fate should threaten her – how absurd! Why, she knew everyone! She had been invited everywhere; her great-grandfather had been governor of one of the Southern States!

She had written to her aunt in India and again in China, receiving no answer. She concluded that her aunt's itinerary had changed, and this was confirmed when a postcard arrived from Honolulu which showed no knowledge of Tom Bowman's death, but announced that she was going with a party to the east coast of Africa. This was a last straw. The languorous and lackadaisical Yanci was on her own at last.

'Why not go to work for a while?' suggested Mr Haedge with some irritation. 'Lots of nice girls do nowadays, just for something to occupy themselves with. There's Elsie Prendergast, who does society news on the *Bulletin*, and that Semple girl –'

'I can't,' said Yanci shortly with a glitter of tears in her eyes. 'I'm going East in February.'

'East? Oh, you're going to visit someone?'

She nodded.

'Yes, I'm going to visit,' she lied, 'so it'd hardly be worthwhile to go to work.' She could have wept, but she managed a haughty look. 'I'd like to try reporting sometime, though, just for the fun of it.'

'Yes, it's quite a lot of fun,' agreed Mr Haedge with some irony. 'Still, I suppose there's no hurry about it. You must have plenty of that thousand dollars left.'

'Oh, plenty!'

There were a few hundred left, she knew.

'Well, then I suppose a good rest, a change of scene would be the best thing for you.'

'Yes,' answered Yanci. Her lips were trembling and she rose, scarcely able to control herself. Mr Haedge seemed so impersonally cold. 'That's why I'm going. A good rest is what I need.'

'I think you're wise.'

What Mr Haedge would have thought had he seen the dozen drafts she wrote that night of a certain letter is problematical. Here are two of the earlier ones. The bracketed words are proposed substitutions:

Dear Scott: Not having seen you since that day I was such a silly ass and wept on your coat, I thought I'd write and tell you that I'm coming East pretty soon and would like you to have lunch [dinner] with me or something. I have been living in a room [suite] at the Hiawatha Hotel, intending to meet my aunt, with whom I am going to live [stay], and who is coming back from China this month [spring]. Meanwhile I have a lot of invitations to visit, etc., in the East, and I thought I would do it now. So I'd like to see you –

This draft ended here and went into the wastebasket. After an hour's work she produced the following:

My dear Mr Kimberly: I have often [sometimes] wondered how you've been since I saw you. I am coming East next month before going to visit my aunt in Chicago, and you must come and see me. I have been going out very little, but my physician advises me that I need a change, so I expect to shock the proprieties by some very gay visits in the East –

Finally in despondent abandon she wrote a simple note without explanation or subterfuge, tore it up and went to bed. Next morning she identified it in the wastebasket, decided it was the best one after all and sent him a fair copy. It ran:

Dear Scott: Just a line to tell you I will be at the Ritz-Carlton Hotel
from February 7th, probably for ten days. If you'll phone me some
rainy afternoon I'll invite you to tea.
Sincerely,
Yanci Bowman.

7

Yanci was going to the Ritz for no more reason than that she had once told Scott Kimberly that she always went there. When she reached New York – a cold New York, a strangely menacing New York, quite different from the gay city of theatres and hotel-corridor rendezvous that she had known – there was exactly two hundred dollars in her purse.

It had taken a large part of her bank account to live, and she had at last broken into her sacred three hundred dollars to substitute pretty and delicate quarter-mourning clothes for the heavy black she had laid away.

Walking into the hotel at the moment when its exquisitely dressed patrons were assembled for luncheon, it drained at her confidence to appear bored and at ease. Surely the clerks at the desk knew the contents of her pocketbook. She fancied even that the bellboys were snickering at the foreign labels she had steamed from an old trunk of her father's and pasted on her suitcase. This last thought horrified her. Perhaps the very hotels and steamers so grandly named had long since been out of commission!

As she stood drumming her fingers on the desk she was wondering whether if she were refused admittance she could muster a casual smile and stroll out coolly enough to deceive two richly dressed women standing near. It had not taken long for the confidence of twenty years to evaporate. Three months without security had made an ineffaceable mark on Yanci's soul.

'Twenty-four sixty-two,' said the clerk callously.

Her heart settled back into place as she followed the bellboy to the elevator, meanwhile casting a nonchalant glance at the two fashionable women as she passed them. Were their skirts long or short? – longer, she noticed.

She wondered how much the skirt of her new walking suit could be let out.

At luncheon her spirits soared. The head waiter bowed to her. The light rattle of conversation, the subdued hum of the music soothed her. She ordered supreme of melon, eggs Suzette and an artichoke, and signed her room number to the cheque with scarcely a glance at it as it lay beside her plate. Up in her room, with the telephone directory open on the bed before her, she tried to locate her scattered metropolitan acquaintances. Yet even as the phone numbers, with their supercilious tags, Plaza, Circle and Rhinelander, stared out at her, she could feel a cold wind blow at her unstable confidence. These girls, acquaintances of school, of a summer, of a house party, even of a weekend at a college prom – what claim or attraction could she, poor and friendless, exercise over them? They had their loves, their dates, their week's gaiety planned in advance. They would almost resent her inconvenient memory.

Nevertheless, she called four girls. One of them was out, one at Palm Beach, one in California. The only one to whom she talked said in a hearty voice that she was in bed with grippe, but would phone Yanci as soon as she felt well enough to go out. Then Yanci gave up the girls. She would have to create the illusion of a good time in some other manner. The illusion must be created – that was part of her plan.

She looked at her watch and found that it was three o'clock. Scott Kimberly should have phoned before this, or at least left some word. Still, he was probably busy – at a club, she thought vaguely, or else buying some neckties. He would probably call at four.

Yanci was well aware that she must work quickly. She had figured to a nicety that one hundred and fifty dollars carefully expended would carry her through two weeks, no more. The idea of failure, the fear that at the end of that time she would be friendless and penniless had not begun to bother her.

It was not the first time that for amusement, for a coveted invitation or for curiosity she had deliberately set out to capture a man, but it was the first time she had laid her plans with necessity and desperation pressing in on her.

One of her strongest cards had always been her background, the impression she gave that she was popular and desired and happy. This she must create now, and apparently out of nothing. Scott must somehow be brought to think that a fair portion of New York was at her feet.

At four she went over to Park Avenue, where the sun was out walking and the February day was fresh and odorous of spring and the high apartments of her desire lined the street with radiant whiteness. Here she would live on a gay schedule of pleasure. In these smart not-to-be-entered-without-a-card women's shops she would spend the morning hours acquiring and acquiring, ceaselessly and without thought of expense; in these restaurants she would lunch at noon in company with other fashionable women, orchid-adorned always, and perhaps bearing an absurdly dwarfed Pomeranian in her sleek arms.

In the summer – well she would go to Tuxedo, perhaps to an immaculate house perched high on a fashionable eminence, where she would emerge to visit a world of teas and balls, of horse shows and polo. Between the halves of the polo game the players would cluster around her in their white suits and helmets, admiringly, and when she swept away, bound for some new delight, she would be followed by the eyes of many envious but intimidated women.

Every other summer they would, of course, go abroad. She began to plan a typical year, distributing a few months here and a few months there until she – and Scott Kimberly, by implication – would become the very auguries of the season, shifting with the slightest stirring of the social barometer from rusticity to urbanity, from palm to pine.

She had two weeks, no more, in which to attain to this position. In an ecstasy of determined emotion she lifted up her head towards the tallest of the tall white apartments.

'It will be too marvellous!' she said to herself.

For almost the first time in her life her words were not too exaggerated to express the wonder shining in her eyes.

8

About five o'clock she hurried back to the hotel, demanding feverishly at the desk if there had been a telephone message for her. To her profound disappointment there was nothing. A minute after she had entered her room the phone rang.

'This is Scott Kimberly.'

At the words a call to battle echoed in her heart.

'Oh, how do you do?'

Her tone implied that she had almost forgotten him. It was not frigid – it was merely casual.

As she answered the inevitable question as to the hour when she had arrived a warm glow spread over her. Now that, from a personification of all the riches and pleasure she craved, he had materialised as merely a male voice over the telephone, her confidence became strengthened. Male voices were male voices. They could be managed; they could be made to intone syllables of which the minds behind them had no approval. Male voices could be made sad or tender or despairing at her will. She rejoiced. The soft clay was ready to her hand.

'Won't you take dinner with me tonight?' Scott was suggesting.

'Why' – perhaps not, she thought; let him think of her tonight – 'I don't believe I'll be able to,' she said. 'I've got an engagement for dinner and the theatre. I'm terribly sorry.'

Her voice did not sound sorry – it sounded polite. Then as though a happy thought had occurred to her as to a time and place where she could work him into her list of dates, 'I'll tell you: why don't you come around here this afternoon and have tea with me?'

He would be there immediately. He had been playing squash and as soon as he took a plunge he would arrive. Yanci hung up the phone and turned with a quiet efficiency to the mirror, too tense to smile.

She regarded her lustrous eyes and dusky hair in critical approval. Then she took a lavender tea gown from her trunk and began to dress.

She let him wait seven minutes in the lobby before she appeared; then she approached him with a friendly, lazy smile.

'How do you do?' she murmured. 'It's marvellous to see you again. How are you?' And, with a long sigh, 'I'm frightfully tired. I've been on

33

the go ever since I got here this morning; shopping and then tearing off to luncheon and a matinée. I've bought everything I saw. I don't know how I'm going to pay for it all.'

She remembered vividly that when they had first met she had told him, without expecting to be believed, how unpopular she was. She could not risk such a remark now, even in jest. He must think that she had been on the go every minute of the day.

They took a table and were served olive sandwiches and tea. He was so good-looking, she thought, and marvellously dressed. His grey eyes regarded her with interest from under immaculate ash-blond hair. She wondered how he passed his days, how he liked her costume, what he was thinking of at that moment.

'How long will you be here?' he asked.

'Well, two weeks, off and on. I'm going down to Princeton for the February prom and then up to a house party in Westchester County for a few days. Are you shocked at me for going out so soon? Father would have wanted me to, you know. He was very modern in all his ideas.'

She had debated this remark on the train. She was not going to a house party. She was not invited to the Princeton prom. Such things, nevertheless, were necessary to create the illusion. That was everything – the illusion.

'And then,' she continued, smiling, 'two of my old beaus are in town, which makes it nice for me.'

She saw Scott blink and she knew that he appreciated the significance of this.

'What are your plans for this winter?' he demanded. 'Are you going back West?'

'No. You see, my aunt returns from India this week. She's going to open her Florida house, and we'll stay there until the middle of March. Then we'll come up to Hot Springs and we may go to Europe for the summer.'

This was all the sheerest fiction. Her first letter to her aunt, which had given the bare details of Tom Bowman's death, had at last reached its destination. Her aunt had replied with a note of conventional sympathy and the announcement that she would be back in America within two years if she didn't decide to live in Italy.

'But you'll let me see something of you while you're here,' urged Scott, after attending to this impressive programme. 'If you can't have dinner with me tonight, how about Wednesday – that's the day after tomorrow?'

'Wednesday? Let's see.' Yanci's brow was knit with imitation thought. 'I think I have a date for Wednesday, but I don't know for certain. How about phoning me tomorrow, and I'll let you know? Because I want to go with you, only I think I've made an engagement.'

'Very well, I'll phone you.'

'Do – about ten.'

'Try to be able to – then or any time.'

'I'll tell you – if I can't go to dinner with you Wednesday I can go to lunch surely.'

'All right,' he agreed. 'And we'll go to a matinée.'

They danced several times. Never by word or sign did Yanci betray more than the most cursory interest in him until just at the end, when she offered him her hand to say goodbye.

'Goodbye, Scott.'

For just the fraction of a second – not long enough for him to be sure it had happened at all, but just enough so that he would be reminded, however faintly, of that night on the Mississippi boulevard – she looked into his eyes. Then she turned quickly and hurried away.

She took her dinner in a little tea room around the corner. It was an economical dinner which cost a dollar and a half. There was no date concerned in it at all, and no man – except an elderly man in spats who tried to speak to her as she came out the door.

9

Sitting alone in one of the magnificent moving-picture theatres – a luxury which she thought she could afford – Yanci watched Mae Murray swirl through splendidly imagined vistas, and meanwhile considered the progress of the first day. In retrospect it was a distinct success. She had given the correct impression both as to her material prosperity and as to her attitude towards Scott himself. It seemed best to avoid evening dates. Let him have the evenings to himself, to think of her, to imagine her with other men, even to spend a few lonely hours in his apartment, considering how much more cheerful it might be if –. Let time and absence work for her.

Engrossed for a while in the moving picture, she calculated the cost of the apartment in which its heroine endured her movie wrongs. She admired its slender Italian table, occupying only one side of the large dining room and flanked by a long bench which gave it an air of medieval luxury. She rejoiced in the beauty of Mae Murray's clothes and furs, her gorgeous hats, her short-seeming French shoes. Then after a moment her mind returned to her own drama; she wondered if Scott were already engaged, and her heart dipped at the thought. Yet it was unlikely. He had been too quick to phone her on her arrival, too lavish with his time, too responsive that afternoon.

After the picture she returned to the Ritz, where she slept deeply and happily for almost the first time in three months. The atmosphere around her no longer seemed cold. Even the floor clerk had smiled kindly and admiringly when Yanci asked for her key.

Next morning at ten Scott phoned. Yanci, who had been up for hours, pretended to be drowsy from her dissipation of the night before.

No, she could not take dinner with him on Wednesday. She was terribly sorry; she had an engagement, as she had feared. But she could have luncheon and go to a matinée if he would get her back in time for tea.

She spent the day roving the streets. On top of a bus, though not on the front seat, where Scott might possibly spy her, she sailed out Riverside Drive and back along Fifth Avenue just at the winter twilight, and her feeling for New York and its gorgeous splendours deepened and redoubled. Here she must live and be rich, be nodded to by the traffic policemen at the corners as she sat in her limousine – with a small dog – and here she must stroll on Sunday to and from a stylish church, with Scott, handsome in his cutaway and tall hat, walking devotedly at her side.

At luncheon on Wednesday she described for Scott's benefit a fanciful two days. She told of a motoring trip up the Hudson and gave her opinion of two plays she had seen with – it was implied – adoring gentlemen beside her. She had read up very carefully on the plays in the morning paper and chosen two concerning which she could garner the most information.

'Oh,' he said in dismay, 'you've seen Dulcy? I have two seats for it – but you won't want to go again.'

'Oh, no, I don't mind,' she protested truthfully. 'You see, we went late, and anyway I adored it.'

But he wouldn't hear of her sitting through it again – besides, he had seen it himself. It was a play Yanci was mad to see, but she was compelled to watch him while he exchanged the tickets for others, and for poor seats available at the last moment. The game seemed difficult at times.

'By the way,' he said afterwards as they drove back to the hotel in a taxi, 'you'll be going down to the Princeton prom tomorrow, won't you?'

She started. She had not realised that it would be so soon or that he would know of it.

'Yes,' she answered coolly. 'I'm going down tomorrow afternoon.'

'On the two-twenty, I suppose,' Scott commented; and then, 'Are you going to meet the boy who's taking you down – at Princeton?'

For an instant she was off her guard.

'Yes, he'll meet the train.'

'Then I'll take you to the station,' proposed Scott. 'There'll be a crowd, and you may have trouble getting a porter.'

She could think of nothing to say, no valid objection to make. She wished she had said that she was going by automobile, but she could conceive of no graceful and plausible way of amending her first admission.

'That's mighty sweet of you.'

'You'll be at the Ritz when you come back?'

'Oh, yes,' she answered. 'I'm going to keep my rooms.'

Her bedroom was the smallest and least expensive in the hotel.

She concluded to let him put her on the train for Princeton; in fact, she saw no alternative. Next day as she packed her suitcase after luncheon the situation had taken such hold of her imagination that she filled it with the very things she would have chosen had she really been going to the prom. Her intention was to get out at the first stop and take the train back to New York.

Scott called for her at half-past one and they took a taxi to the Pennsylvania Station. The train was crowded as he had expected, but he found her a seat and stowed her grip in the rack overhead.

'I'll call you Friday to see how you've behaved,' he said.

'All right. I'll be good.'

Their eyes met and in an instant, with an inexplicable, only half-conscious rush of emotion, they were in perfect communion. When Yanci came back, the glance seemed to say, 'Ah, then –'

A voice startled her ear:

'Why, Yanci!'

Yanci looked around. To her horror she recognised a girl named Ellen Harley, one of those to whom she had phoned upon her arrival.

'Well, Yanci Bowman! You're the last person I ever expected to see. How are you?'

Yanci introduced Scott. Her heart was beating violently.

'Are you coming to the prom? How perfectly slick!' cried Ellen. 'Can I sit here with you? I've been wanting to see you. Who are you going with?'

'No one you know.'

'Maybe I do.'

Her words, falling like sharp claws on Yanci's sensitive soul, were interrupted by an unintelligible outburst from the conductor. Scott bowed to Ellen, cast at Yanci one level glance and then hurried off.

The train started. As Ellen arranged her grip and threw off her fur coat Yanci looked around her. The car was gay with girls whose excited chatter filled the damp, rubbery air like smoke. Here and there sat a chaperon, a mass of decaying rock in a field of flowers, predicting with a mute and sombre fatality the end of all gaiety and all youth. How many times had Yanci herself been one of such a crowd, careless and happy, dreaming of the men she would meet, of the battered hacks waiting at the station, the snow-covered campus, the big open fires in the clubhouses, and the imported orchestra beating out defiant melody against the approach of morning.

And now – she was an intruder, uninvited, undesired. As at the Ritz on the day of her arrival, she felt that at any instant her mask would be torn from her and she would be exposed as a pretender to the gaze of all the car.

'Tell me everything!' Ellen was saying. 'Tell me what you've been doing. I didn't see you at any of the football games last fall.'

This was by way of letting Yanci know that she had attended them herself.

The conductor was bellowing from the rear of the car, 'Manhattan Transfer next stop!'

Yanci's cheeks burned with shame. She wondered what she had best do – meditating a confession, deciding against it, answering Ellen's chatter in frightened monosyllables – then, as with an ominous thunder of brakes the speed of the train began to slacken, she sprang on a despairing impulse to her feet.

'My heavens!' she cried. 'I've forgotten my shoes! I've got to go back and get them.'

Ellen reacted to this with annoying efficiency.

'I'll take your suitcase,' she said quickly, 'and you can call for it. I'll be at the Charter Club.'

'No!' Yanci almost shrieked. 'It's got my dress in it!'

Ignoring the lack of logic in her own remark, she swung the suitcase off the rack with what seemed to her a superhuman effort and went reeling down the aisle, stared at curiously by the arrogant eyes of many girls. When she reached the platform just as the train came to a stop she felt weak and shaken. She stood on the hard cement which marks the quaint old village of Manhattan Transfer and tears were streaming down her cheeks as she watched the unfeeling cars speed off to Princeton with their burden of happy youth.

After half an hour's wait Yanci got on a train and returned to New York. In thirty minutes she had lost the confidence that a week had gained for her. She came back to her little room and lay down quietly upon the bed.

10

By Friday Yanci's spirits had partly recovered from their chill depression. Scott's voice over the telephone in mid-morning was like a tonic, and she told him of the delights of Princeton with convincing enthusiasm, drawing vicariously upon a prom she had attended there two years before. He was anxious to see her, he said. Would she come to dinner and the theatre that night? Yanci considered, greatly tempted. Dinner – she had been economising on meals, and a gorgeous dinner in some extravagant showplace followed by a musical comedy appealed to her starved fancy, indeed; but instinct told her that the time was not yet right. Let him wait. Let him dream a little more, a little longer.

'I'm too tired, Scott,' she said with an air of extreme frankness; 'that's the whole truth of the matter. I've been out every night since I've been here, and I'm really half dead. I'll rest up on this house party over the weekend and then I'll go to dinner with you any day you want me.'

There was a minute's silence while she held the phone expectantly.

'Lot of resting up you'll do on a house party,' he replied; 'and, anyway, next week is so far off. I'm awfully anxious to see you, Yanci.'

'So am I, Scott.'

She allowed the faintest caress to linger on his name. When she had hung up she felt happy again. Despite her humiliation on the train her plan had been a success. The illusion was still intact; it was nearly complete. And in three meetings and half a dozen telephone calls she had managed to create a tenser atmosphere between them than if he had seen her constantly in the moods and avowals and beguilements of an out-and-out flirtation.

When Monday came she paid for her first week's hotel bill. The size of it did not alarm her – she was prepared for that – but the shock of seeing so much money go, of realising that there remained only one hundred and twenty dollars of her father's present, gave her a peculiar sinking sensation in the pit of her stomach. She decided to bring guile to bear immediately, to tantalise Scott by a carefully planned incident, and then at the end of the week to show him simply and definitely that she loved him.

As a decoy for Scott's tantalisation she located by telephone a certain

Jimmy Long, a handsome boy with whom she had played as a little girl and who had recently come to New York to work. Jimmy Long was deftly manoeuvred into asking her to go to a matinée with him on Wednesday afternoon. He was to meet her in the lobby at two.

On Wednesday she lunched with Scott. His eyes followed her every motion, and knowing this she felt a great rush of tenderness towards him. Desiring at first only what he represented, she had begun half unconsciously to desire him also. Nevertheless, she did not permit herself the slightest relaxation on that account. The time was too short and the odds too great. That she was beginning to love him only fortified her resolve.

'Where are you going this afternoon?' he demanded.

'To a matinée – with an annoying man.'

'Why is he annoying?'

'Because he wants me to marry him and I don't believe I want to.'

There was just the faintest emphasis on the word 'believe'. The implication was that she was not sure – that is, not quite.

'Don't marry him.'

'I won't – probably.'

'Yanci,' he said in a low voice, 'do you remember a night on that boulevard –'

She changed the subject. It was noon and the room was full of sunlight. It was not quite the place, the time. When he spoke she must have every aspect of the situation in control. He must say only what she wanted said; nothing else would do.

'It's five minutes to two,' she told him, looking at her wristwatch. 'We'd better go. I've got to keep my date.'

'Do you want to go?'

'No,' she answered simply.

This seemed to satisfy him, and they walked out to the lobby. Then Yanci caught sight of a man waiting there, obviously ill at ease and dressed as no habitué of the Ritz ever was. The man was Jimmy Long, not long since a favoured beau of his Western city. And now – his hat was green, actually! His coat, seasons old, was quite evidently the product of a well-known ready-made concern. His shoes, long and narrow, turned up at the toes. From head to foot everything that could possibly be wrong about him was wrong. He was embarrassed by instinct only, unconscious of his gaucherie, an obscene spectre, a nemesis, a horror.

'Hello, Yanci!' he cried, starting towards her with evident relief.

With a heroic effort Yanci turned to Scott, trying to hold his glance to herself. In the very act of turning she noticed the impeccability of Scott's coat, his tie.

'Thanks for luncheon,' she said with a radiant smile. 'See you to-morrow.'

Then she dived rather than ran for Jimmy Long, disposed of his outstretched hand and bundled him bumping through the revolving door with only a quick 'Let's hurry!' to appease his somewhat sulky astonishment.

The incident worried her. She consoled herself by remembering that Scott had had only a momentary glance at the man, and that he had probably been looking at her anyhow. Nevertheless, she was horrified, and it is to be doubted whether Jimmy Long enjoyed her company enough to compensate him for the cut-price, twentieth-row tickets he had obtained at Black's Drug Store.

But if Jimmy as a decoy had proved a lamentable failure, an occurrence of Thursday offered her considerable satisfaction and paid tribute to her quickness of mind. She had invented an engagement for luncheon, and Scott was going to meet her at two o'clock to take her to the Hippodrome. She lunched alone somewhat imprudently in the Ritz dining room and sauntered out almost side by side with a good-looking young man who had been at the table next to her. She expected to meet Scott in the outer lobby, but as she reached the entrance to the restaurant she saw him standing not far away.

On a lightning impulse she turned to the good-looking man abreast of her, bowed sweetly and said in an audible, friendly voice, 'Well, I'll see you later.'

Then before he could even register astonishment she faced about quickly and joined Scott.

'Who was that?' he asked, frowning.

'Isn't he darling-looking?'

'If you like that sort of looks.'

Scott's tone implied that the gentleman referred to was effete and overdressed. Yanci laughed, impersonally admiring the skilfulness of her ruse.

It was in preparation for that all-important Saturday night that on Thursday she went into a shop on Forty-second Street to buy some long gloves. She made her purchase and handed the clerk a fifty-dollar bill so that her lightened pocketbook would feel heavier with the change she could put in. To her surprise the clerk tendered her the package and a twenty-five cent piece.

'Is there anything else?'

'The rest of my change.'

'You've got it. You gave me five dollars. Four-seventy-five for the gloves leaves twenty-five cents.'

'I gave you fifty dollars.'

'You must be mistaken.'

Yanci searched her purse.

'I gave you fifty!' she repeated frantically.

'No, ma'am, I saw it myself.'

They glared at each other in hot irritation. A cash girl was called to testify, then the floor manager; a small crowd gathered.

'Why, I'm perfectly sure!' cried Yanci, two angry tears trembling in her eyes. 'I'm positive!'

The floor manager was sorry, but the lady really must have left it at home. There was no fifty-dollar bill in the cash drawer. The bottom was creaking out of Yanci's rickety world.

'If you'll leave your address,' said the floor manager, 'I'll let you know if anything turns up.'

'Oh, you damn fools!' cried Yanci, losing control. 'I'll get the police!'

And weeping like a child she left the shop. Outside, helplessness overpowered her. How could she prove anything? It was after six and the store was closing even as she left it. Whichever employee had the fifty-dollar bill would be on her way home now before the police could arrive, and why should the New York police believe her, or even give her fair play?

In despair she returned to the Ritz, where she searched through her trunk for the bill with hopeless and mechanical gestures. It was not there. She had known it would not be there. She gathered every penny together and found that she had fifty-one dollars and thirty cents. Telephoning the office, she asked that her bill be made out up to the following noon – she was too dispirited to think of leaving before then.

She waited in her room, not daring even to send for ice water. Then the phone rang and she heard the room clerk's voice, cheerful and metallic.

'Miss Bowman?'

'Yes.'

'Your bill, including tonight, is ex-act-ly fifty-one twenty.'

'Fifty-one twenty?' Her voice was trembling.

'Yes ma'am.'

'Thank you very much.'

Breathless, she sat there beside the telephone, too frightened now to cry. She had ten cents left in the world!

11

Friday. She had scarcely slept. There were dark rings under her eyes, and even a hot bath followed by a cold one failed to arouse her from a despairing lethargy. She had never fully realised what it would mean to be without money in New York; her determination and vitality seemed to have vanished at last with her fifty-dollar bill. There was no help for it now – she must attain her desire today or never.

She was to meet Scott at the Plaza for tea. She wondered – was it her imagination, or had his manner been consciously cool the afternoon before? For the first time in several days she had needed to make no effort to keep the conversation from growing sentimental. Suppose he had decided that it must come to nothing – that she was too extravagant, too frivolous. A hundred eventualities presented themselves to her during the morning – a dreary morning, broken only by her purchase of a ten-cent bun at a grocery store.

It was her first food in twenty hours, but she self-consciously pretended to the grocer to be having an amusing and facetious time in buying one bun. She even asked to see his grapes, but told him, after looking at them appraisingly – and hungrily – that she didn't think she'd buy any. They didn't look ripe to her, she said. The store was full of prosperous women who, with thumb and first finger joined and held high in front of them, were inspecting food. Yanci would have liked to ask one of them for a bunch of grapes. Instead she went up to her room in the hotel and ate her bun.

When four o'clock came she found that she was thinking more about the sandwiches she would have for tea than of what must occur there, and as she walked slowly up Fifth Avenue towards the Plaza she felt a sudden faintness which she took several deep breaths of air to overcome. She wondered vaguely where the breadline was. That was where people in her condition should go – but where was it? How did one find out? She imagined fantastically that it was in the phone book under *B*, or perhaps under *N*, for New York Bread Line.

She reached the Plaza. Scott's figure, as he stood waiting for her in the crowded lobby, was a personification of solidity and hope.

'Let's hurry!' she cried with a tortured smile. 'I feel rather punk and I want some tea.'

She ate a club sandwich, some chocolate ice cream and six tea biscuits. She could have eaten much more, but she dared not. The eventuality of her hunger having been disposed of, she must turn at bay now and face this business of life, represented by the handsome young man who sat opposite her with some emotion whose import she could not determine just behind his level eyes.

But the words, the glance, subtle, pervasive and sweet, that she had planned, failed somehow to come.

'Oh, Scott,' she said in a low voice, 'I'm so tired.'

'Tired of what?' he asked coolly.

'Of – everything.'

There was a silence.

'I'm afraid,' she said uncertainly – 'I'm afraid I won't be able to keep that date with you tomorrow.'

There was no pretence in her voice now. The emotion was apparent in the waver of each word, without intention or control.

'I'm going away.'

'Are you? Where?'

His tone showed a strong interest, but she winced as she saw that that was all.

'My aunt's come back. She wants me to join her in Florida right away.'

'Isn't this rather unexpected?'

'Yes.'

'You'll be coming back soon?' he said after a moment.

'I don't think so. I think we'll go to Europe from – New Orleans.'

'Oh!'

Again there was a pause. It lengthened. In the shadow of a moment it would become awkward, she knew. She had lost – well? Yet, she would go on to the end.

'Will you miss me?'

'Yes.'

One word. She caught his eyes, wondered for a moment if she saw more there than that kindly interest; then she dropped her own again.

'I like it – here at the Plaza,' she heard herself saying.

They spoke of things like that. Afterwards she could never remember what they said. They spoke – even of the tea, of the thaw that was ended and the cold coming down outside. She was sick at heart and she seemed to herself very old. She rose at last.

'I've got to tear,' she said. 'I'm going out to dinner.'

To the last she would keep on – the illusion, that was the important thing. To hold her proud lies inviolate – there was only a moment now. They walked towards the door.

'Put me in a taxi,' she said quietly. 'I don't feel equal to walking.'

He helped her in. They shook hands.

'Goodbye, Scott,' she said.

'Goodbye, Yanci,' he answered slowly.

'You've been awfully nice to me. I'll always remember what a good time you helped to give me this two weeks.'

'The pleasure was mine. Shall I tell the driver the Ritz?'

'No. Just tell him to drive out Fifth. I'll tap on the glass when I want him to stop.'

Out Fifth! He would think, perhaps, that she was dining on Fifth. What an appropriate finish that would be! She wondered if he were impressed. She could not see his face clearly, because the air was dark with the snow and her own eyes were blurred by tears.

'Goodbye,' he said simply.

He seemed to realise that any pretence of sorrow on his part would be transparent. She knew that he did not want her.

The door slammed, the car started, skidding in the snowy street.

Yanci leant back dismally in the corner. Try as she might, she could not see where she had failed or what it was that had changed his attitude towards her. For the first time in her life she had ostensibly offered herself to a man – and he had not wanted her. The precariousness of her position paled beside the tragedy of her defeat.

She let the car go on – the cold air was what she needed, of course. Ten minutes had slipped away dreamily before she realised that she had not a penny with which to pay the driver.

'It doesn't matter,' she thought. 'They'll just send me to jail, and that's a place to sleep.'

She began thinking of the taxi driver.

'He'll be mad when he finds out, poor man. Maybe he's very poor, and he'll have to pay the fare himself.' With a vague sentimentality she began to cry.

'Poor taxi man,' she was saying half aloud. 'Oh, people have such a hard time – such a hard time!'

She rapped on the window and when the car drew up at a kerb she got out. She was at the end of Fifth Avenue and it was dark and cold.

'Send for the police!' she cried in a quick low voice. 'I haven't any money!'

The taxi man scowled down at her.

'Then what'd you get in for?'

She had not noticed that another car had stopped about twenty-five feet behind them. She heard running footsteps in the snow and then a voice at her elbow.

'It's all right,' someone was saying to the taxi man. 'I've got it right here.'

A bill was passed up. Yanci slumped sideways against Scott's overcoat.

Scott knew – he knew because he had gone to Princeton to surprise her, because the stranger she had spoken to in the Ritz had been his best friend, because the cheque of her father's for three hundred dollars had been returned to him marked 'No funds'. Scott knew – he had known for days.

But he said nothing; only stood there holding her with one arm as her taxi drove away.

'Oh, it's you,' said Yanci faintly. 'Lucky you came along. I left my purse back at the Ritz, like an awful fool. I do such ridiculous things –'

Scott laughed with some enjoyment. There was a light snow falling, and lest she should slip in the damp he picked her up and carried her back towards his waiting taxi.

'Such ridiculous things,' she repeated.

'Go to the Ritz first,' he said to the driver. 'I want to get a trunk.'

Love in the Night

1

The words thrilled Val. They had come into his mind sometime during the fresh gold April afternoon and he kept repeating them to himself over and over: 'Love in the night; love in the night.' He tried them in three languages – Russian, French and English – and decided that they were best in English. In each language they meant a different sort of love and a different sort of night – the English night seemed the warmest and softest with a thinnest and most crystalline sprinkling of stars. The English love seemed the most fragile and romantic – a white dress and a dim face above it and eyes that were pools of light. And when I add that it was a French night he was thinking about, after all, I see I must go back and begin over.

Val was half Russian and half American. His mother was the daughter of that Morris Hasylton who helped finance the Chicago World's Fair in 1892, and his father was – see the Almanach de Gotha[3], issue of 1910 – Prince Paul Serge Boris Rostov, son of Prince Vladimir Rostov, grandson of a grand duke – 'Jimber-jawed Serge' – and third-cousin-once-removed to the Tsar. It was all very impressive, you see, on that side – house in St Petersburg, shooting lodge near Riga, and swollen villa, more like a palace, overlooking the Mediterranean. It was at this villa in Cannes that the Rostovs passed the winter – and it wasn't at all the thing to remind Princess Rostov that this Riviera villa, from the marble fountain – after Bernini[4] – to the gold cordial glasses – after dinner – was paid for with American gold.

The Russians, of course, were gay people on the Continent in the gala days before the War. Of the three races that used Southern France for a pleasure ground they were easily the most adept at the grand manner. The English were too practical, and the Americans, though they spent freely, had no tradition of romantic conduct. But the Russians – there was a people as gallant as the Latins, and rich besides! When the Rostovs arrived at Cannes late in January the restaurateurs telegraphed north for the Prince's favourite labels to paste on their champagne, and the jewellers put incredibly gorgeous articles aside to show to him – but not to the princess – and the Russian Church was swept and garnished for the season that the Prince might beg orthodox forgiveness for his sins. Even the Mediterranean turned obligingly to a deep wine colour in the spring evening, and fishing boats with robin-breasted sails loitered exquisitely offshore.

In a vague way young Val realised that this was all for the benefit of him and his family. It was a privileged paradise, this white little city on the water, in which he was free to do what he liked because he was rich and young and the blood of Peter the Great ran indigo in his veins. He was only seventeen in 1914, when this history begins, but he had already fought a duel with a young man four years his senior, and he had a small hairless scar to show for it on top of his handsome head.

But the question of love in the night was the thing nearest his heart. It was a vague pleasant dream he had, something that was going to happen to him some day that would be unique and incomparable. He could have told no more about it than that there was a lovely unknown girl concerned in it, and that it ought to take place beneath the Riviera moon.

The odd thing about all this was not that he had this excited and yet almost spiritual hope of romance, for all boys of any imagination have just such hopes, but that it actually came true. And when it happened, it happened so unexpectedly; it was such a jumble of impressions and emotions, of curious phrases that sprang to his lips, of sights and sounds and moments that were here, were lost, were past, that he scarcely understood it at all. Perhaps its very vagueness preserved it in his heart and made him forever unable to forget.

There was an atmosphere of love all about him that spring – his father's loves, for instance, which were many and indiscreet, and which Val became aware of gradually from overhearing the gossip of servants, and definitely from coming on his American mother unexpectedly one afternoon, to find her storming hysterically at his father's picture on the salon wall. In the picture his father wore a white uniform with a furred dolman and looked back impassively at his wife as if to say, 'Were you under the impression, my dear, that you were marrying into a family of clergymen?'

Val tiptoed away, surprised, confused – and excited. It didn't shock him as it would have shocked an American boy of his age. He had known for years what life was among the Continental rich, and he condemned his father only for making his mother cry.

Love went on around him – reproachless love and illicit love alike. As he strolled along the seaside promenade at nine o'clock, when the stars were bright enough to compete with the bright lamps, he was aware of love on every side. From the open-air cafés, vivid with dresses just down from Paris, came a sweet pungent odour of flowers and chartreuse and fresh black coffee and cigarettes – and mingled with them all he caught another scent, the mysterious thrilling scent of love. Hands touched jewel-sparkling hands upon the white tables. Gay dresses and white shirt-fronts swayed together, and matches were held, trembling a little, for slow-lighting cigarettes. On the other side of the boulevard lovers less fashionable, young Frenchmen who worked in the stores of Cannes, sauntered with their fiancées under the dim trees, but Val's young eyes seldom turned that way. The luxury of music and bright colours and low voices – they were all part of his dream. They were the essential trappings of love in the night.

But assume as he might the rather fierce expression that was expected from a Russian gentleman who walked the streets alone, Val was beginning to be unhappy. April twilight had succeeded March twilight, the season was almost over, and he had found no use to make of the warm spring evenings. The girls of sixteen and seventeen whom he knew, were chaperoned with care between dusk and bedtime – this, remember was before the War – and the others who might gladly have walked beside him were an affront to his romantic desire. So April passed by – one week, two weeks, three weeks…

He had played tennis until seven and loitered at the courts for another hour, so it was half-past eight when a tired cab horse accomplished the hill on which gleamed the façade of the Rostov villa. The lights of his mother's limousine were yellow in the drive, and the Princess, buttoning her gloves, was just coming out the glowing door. Val tossed two francs to the cabman and went to kiss her on the cheek.

'Don't touch me,' she said quickly. 'You've been handling money.'

'But not in my mouth, Mother,' he protested humorously.

The Princess looked at him impatiently.

'I'm angry,' she said. 'Why must you be so late tonight? We're dining on a yacht and you were to have come along too.'

'What yacht?'

'Americans.' There was always a faint irony in her voice when she mentioned the land of her nativity. Her America was the Chicago of the Nineties which she still thought of as the vast upstairs to a butcher shop. Even the irregularities of Prince Paul were not too high a price to have paid for her escape.

'Two yachts,' she continued; 'in fact we don't know which one. The note was very indefinite. Very careless indeed.'

Americans. Val's mother had taught him to look down on Americans, but she hadn't succeeded in making him dislike them. American men noticed you, even if you were seventeen. He liked Americans. Although he was thoroughly Russian he wasn't immaculately so – the exact proportion, like that of a celebrated soap, was about ninety-nine and three-quarters per cent.

'I want to come,' he said, 'I'll hurry up, Mother. I'll –'

'We're late now.' The Princess turned as her husband appeared in the door. 'Now Val says he wants to come.'

'He can't,' said Prince Paul shortly. 'He's too outrageously late.'

Val nodded. Russian aristocrats, however indulgent about themselves, were always admirably spartan about their children. There were no arguments.

'I'm sorry,' he said.

Prince Paul grunted. The footman, in red and silver livery, opened the limousine door. But the grunt decided the matter for Val, because Princess Rostov at that day and hour had certain grievances against her husband which gave her command of the domestic situation.

'On second thought you'd better come, Val,' she announced coolly. 'It's too late now, but come after dinner. The yacht is either the *Minnehaha* or the *Privateer*.' She got into the limousine. 'The one to come :o will be the gayer one, I suppose – the Jackson's yacht –'

'Find got sense,' muttered the Prince cryptically, conveying that Val would find it if he had any sense. 'Have my man take a look at you 'fore you start. Wear tie of mine 'stead of that outrageous string you affected in Vienna. Grow up. High time.'

As the limousine crawled crackling down the pebbled drive Val's face was burning.

2

It was dark in Cannes harbour, rather it seemed dark after the brightness of the promenade that Val had just left behind. Three frail dock lights glittered dimly upon innumerable fishing boats heaped like shells along the beach. Further out in the water there were other lights where a fleet of slender yachts rode the tide with slow dignity, and further still a full ripe moon made the water bosom into a polished dancing floor. Occasionally there was a 'swish! creak! drip!' as a row-boat moved about in the shallows, and its blurred shape threaded the labyrinth of hobbled fishing skiffs and launches. Val, descending the velvet slope of sand, stumbled over a sleeping boatman and caught the rank savour of garlic and plain wine. Taking the man by the shoulders he shook open his startled eyes.

'Do you know where the *Minnehaha* is anchored, and the *Privateer*?'

As they slid out into the bay he lay back in the stern and stared with vague discontent at the Riviera moon. That was the right moon, all right. Frequently, five nights out of seven, there was the right moon. And here was the soft air, aching with enchantment, and here was the music, many strains of music from many orchestras, drifting out from the shore. Eastward lay the dark Cape of Antibes, and then Nice, and beyond that Monte Carlo, where the night rang chinking full of gold. Some day he would enjoy all that, too, know its every pleasure and success – when he was too old and wise to care.

But tonight – tonight, that stream of silver that waved like a wide strand of curly hair towards the moon; those soft romantic lights of Cannes behind him, the irresistable ineffable love in this air – that was to be wasted for ever.

'Which one?' asked the boatman suddenly.

'Which what?' demanded Val, sitting up.

'Which boat?'

He pointed. Val turned; above hovered the grey, sword-like prow of a yacht. During the long sustained longing of his wish they had covered half a mile.

He read the brass letters over his head. It was the *Privateer*, but there were only dim lights on board, and no music and no voices, only a murmurous 'k-plash' at intervals as the small waves leapt at the sides.

'The other one,' said Val; 'the *Minnehaha*.'

'Don't go yet.'

Val started. The voice, low and soft, had dropped down from the darkness overhead.

'What's the hurry?' said the soft voice. 'Thought maybe somebody was coming to see me, and have suffered terrible disappointment.'

The boatman lifted his oars and looked hesitatingly at Val. But Val was silent, so the man let the blades fall into the water and swept the boat out into the moonlight.

'Wait a minute!' cried Val sharply.

'Goodbye,' said the voice. 'Come again when you can stay longer.'

'But I am going to stay now,' he answered breathlessly.

He gave the necessary order and the rowboat swung back to the foot of the small companionway. Someone young, someone in a misty white dress, someone with a lovely low voice, had actually called to him out of the velvet dark. 'If she has eyes!' Val murmured to himself. He liked the romantic sound of it and repeated it under his breath – 'If she has eyes.'

'What are you?' She was directly above him now; she was looking down and he was looking up as he climbed the ladder, and as their eyes met they both began to laugh.

She was very young, slim, almost frail, with a dress that accentuated her youth by its blanched simplicity. Two wan dark spots on her cheeks marked where the colour was by day.

'What are you?' she repeated, moving back and laughing again as his head appeared on the level of the deck. 'I'm frightened now and I want to know.'

'I am a gentleman,' said Val, bowing.

'What sort of a gentleman? There are all sorts of gentlemen. There was a – there was a coloured gentleman at the table next to ours in Paris, and so –' She broke off. 'You're not American, are you?'

'I'm Russian,' he said, as he might have announced himself to be an archangel. He thought quickly and then added, 'And I am the most fortunate of Russians. All this day, all this spring I have dreamt of falling in love on such a night, and now I see that heaven has sent me to you.'

'Just one moment!' she said, with a little gasp. 'I'm sure now that this visit is a mistake. I don't go in for anything like that. Please!'

'I beg your pardon.' He looked at her in bewilderment, unaware that he had taken too much for granted. Then he drew himself up formally. 'I have made an error. If you will excuse me I will say goodnight.'

He turned away. His hand was on the rail.

'Don't go,' she said, pushing a strand of indefinite hair out of her eyes. 'On second thoughts you can talk any nonsense you like if you'll only not go. I'm miserable and I don't want to be left alone.'

Val hesitated; there was some element in this that he failed to understand. He had taken it for granted that a girl who called to a strange man at night, even from the deck of a yacht, was certainly in a mood for romance. And he wanted intensely to stay. Then he remembered that this was one of the two yachts he had been seeking.

'I imagine that the dinner's on the other boat,' he said.

'The dinner? Oh, yes, it's on the *Minnehaha*. Were you going there?'

'I was going there – a long time ago.'

'What's your name?'

He was on the point of telling her when something made him ask a question instead.

'And you? Why are you not at the party?'

'Because I preferred to stay here. Mrs Jackson said there would be some Russians there – I suppose that's you.' She looked at him with interest. 'You're a very young man, aren't you?'

'I am much older than I look,' said Val stiffly. 'People always comment on it. It's considered rather a remarkable thing.'

'How old are you?'

'Twenty-one,' he lied.

She laughed.

'What nonsense! You're not more than nineteen.'

His annoyance was so perceptible that she hastened to reassure him. 'Cheer up! I'm only seventeen myself. I might have gone to the party if I'd thought there'd be anyone under fifty there.'

He welcomed the change of subject.

'You preferred to sit and dream here beneath the moon.'

'I've been thinking of mistakes.' They sat down side by side in two canvas deckchairs. 'It's a most engrossing subject – the subject of mistakes. Women seldom brood about mistakes – they're much more willing to forget them than men are. But when they do brood –'

'You have made a mistake?' enquired Val.

She nodded.

'Is it something that cannot be repaired?'

'I think so,' she answered. 'I can't be sure. That's what I was considering when you came along.'

'Perhaps I can help you in some way,' said Val. 'Perhaps your mistake is not irreparable, after all.'

'You can't,' she said unhappily. 'So let's not think about it. I'm very tired of my mistake and I'd much rather you'd tell me about all the gay, cheerful things that are going on in Cannes tonight.'

They glanced shoreward at the line of mysterious and alluring lights, the big toy banks with candles inside that were really the great fashionable hotels, the lighted clock in the old town, the blurred glow of the Café de Paris, the pricked-out points of villa windows rising on slow hills towards the dark sky.

'What is everyone doing there?' she whispered. 'It looks as though something gorgeous was going on, but what it is I can't quite tell.'

'Everyone there is making love,' said Val quietly.

'Is that it?' She looked for a long time, with a strange expression in her eyes. 'Then I want to go home to America,' she said. 'There is too much love here. I want to go home tomorrow.'

'You are afraid of being in love then?'

She shook her head.

'It isn't that. It's just because – there is no love here for me.'

'Or for me either,' added Val quietly. 'It is sad that we two should be at such a lovely place on such a lovely night and have – nothing.'

He was leaning towards her intently, with a sort of inspired and chaste romance in his eyes – and she drew back.

'Tell me more about yourself,' she enquired quickly. 'If you are Russian where did you learn to speak such excellent English?'

'My mother was American,' he admitted. 'My grandfather was American also, so she had no choice in the matter.'

'Then you're American too!'

'I am Russian,' said Val with dignity.

She looked at him closely, smiled and decided not to argue. 'Well then,' she said diplomatically, 'I suppose you must have a Russian name.'

But he had no intention now of telling her his name. A name, even the Rostov name, would be a desecration of the night. They were their own low voices, their two white faces – and that was enough. He was sure, without any reason for being sure but with a sort of instinct that sang triumphantly through his mind, that in a little while, a minute or an hour, he was going to undergo an initiation into the life of romance. His name had no reality beside what was stirring in his heart.

'You are beautiful,' he said suddenly.

'How do you know?'

'Because for women moonlight is the hardest light of all.'

'Am I nice in the moonlight?'

'You are the loveliest thing that I have ever known.'

'Oh.' She thought this over. 'Of course I had no business to let you come on board. I might have known what we'd talk about – in this moon. But I can't sit here and look at the shore – for ever. I'm too young for that. Don't you think I'm too young for that?'

'Much too young,' he agreed solemnly.

Suddenly they both became aware of new music that was close at hand, music that seemed to come out of the water not a hundred yards away.

'Listen!' she cried. 'It's from the *Minnehaha*. They've finished dinner.'

For a moment they listened in silence.

'Thank you,' said Val suddenly.

'For what?'

He hardly knew he had spoken. He was thanking the deep low horns for singing in the breeze, the sea for its warm murmurous complaint against the bow, the milk of the stars for washing over them until he felt buoyed up in a substance more taut than air.

'So lovely,' she whispered.

'What are we going to do about it?'

'Do we have to do something about it? I thought we could just sit and enjoy –'

'You didn't think that,' he interrupted quietly. 'You know that we must do something about it. I am going to make love to you – and you are going to be glad.'

'I can't,' she said very low. She wanted to laugh now, to make some light cool remark that would bring the situation back into the safe waters of a casual flirtation. But it was too late now. Val knew that the music had completed what the moon had begun.

'I will tell you the truth,' he said. 'You are my first love. I am seventeen – the same age as you, no more.'

There was something utterly disarming about the fact that they were the same age. It made her helpless before the fate that had thrown them together. The deckchairs creaked and he was conscious of a faint illusive perfume as they swayed suddenly and childishly together.

3

Whether he kissed her once or several times he could not afterwards remember, though it must have been an hour that they sat there close together and he held her hand. What surprised him most about making love was that it seemed to have no element of wild passion – regret, desire, despair – but a delirious promise of such happiness in the world, in living, as he had never known. First love – this was only first love! What must love itself in its fullness, its perfection be. He did not know that what he was experiencing then – that unreal, undesirous medley of ecstasy and peace – would be unrecapturable for ever.

The music ceased for some time when presently the murmurous silence was broken by the sound of a rowboat disturbing the quiet waves. She sprang suddenly to her feet and her eyes strained out over the bay.

'Listen!' she said quickly. 'I want you to tell me your name.'

'No.'

'Please,' she begged him. 'I'm going away tomorrow.'

He didn't answer.

'I don't want you to forget me,' she said. 'My name is –'

'I won't forget you. I will promise to remember you always. Whoever I may love I will always compare her to you, my first love. So long as I live you will always have that much freshness in my heart.'

'I want you to remember,' she murmured brokenly. 'Oh, this has meant more to me than it has to you – much more.'

She was standing so close to him that he felt her warm young breath on his face. Once again they swayed together. He pressed her hands and wrists between his as it seemed the right thing to do, and kissed her lips. It was the right kiss, he thought, the romantic kiss – not too little or too much. Yet there was a sort of promise in it of other kisses he might have had, and it was with a slight sinking of his heart that he heard the rowboat close to the yacht and realised that his family had returned. The evening was over.

'And this is only the beginning,' he told himself. 'All my life will be like this night.'

She was saying something in a low quick voice and he was listening tensely.

'You must know one thing – I am married. Three months ago. That was the mistake that I was thinking about when the moon brought you out here. In a moment you will understand.'

She broke off as the boat swung against the companionway and a man's voice floated up out of the darkness.

'Is that you, my dear?'

'Yes.'

'What is this other rowboat waiting?'

'One of Mrs Jackson's guests came here by mistake and I made him stay and amuse me for an hour.'

A moment later the thin white hair and weary face of a man of sixty appeared above the level of the deck. And then Val saw and realised too late how much he cared.

4

When the Riviera season ended in May the Rostovs and all the other Russians closed their villas and went north for the summer. The

Russian Orthodox Church was locked up and so were the bins of rarer wine, and the fashionable spring moonlight was put away, so to speak, to wait for their return.

'We'll be back next season,' they said as a matter of course.

But this was premature, for they were never coming back any more. Those few who straggled south again after five tragic years were glad to get work as chambermaids or *valets de chambre* in the great hotels where they had once dined. Many of them, of course, were killed in the War or in the Revolution; many of them faded out as spongers and small cheats in the big capitals, and not a few ended their lives in a sort of stupefied despair.

When the Kerensky Government[5] collapsed in 1917, Val was a lieutenant on the Eastern Front, trying desperately to enforce authority in his company long after any vestige of it remained. He was still trying when Prince Paul Rostov and his wife gave up their lives one rainy morning to atone for the blunders of the Romanovs – and the enviable career of Morris Hasylton's daughter ended in a city that bore even more resemblance to a butcher shop than had Chicago in 1892.

After that Val fought with Denikin's army[6] for a while until he realised that he was participating in a hollow farce and the glory of Imperial Russia was over. Then he went to France and was suddenly confronted with the astounding problem of keeping his body and soul together.

It was, of course, natural that he should think of going to America. Two vague aunts with whom his mother had quarrelled many years ago still lived there in comparative affluence. But the idea was repugnant to the prejudices his mother had implanted in him, and besides he hadn't sufficient money left to pay for his passage over. Until a possible counter-revolution should restore to him the Rostov properties in Russia he must somehow keep alive in France.

So he went to the little city he knew best of all. He went to Cannes. His last two hundred francs bought him a third-class ticket and when he arrived he gave his dress suit to an obliging party who dealt in such things and received in return money for food and bed. He was sorry afterwards that he had sold the dress suit, because it might have helped him to a position as a waiter. But he obtained work as a taxi driver instead and was quite as happy, or rather quite as miserable, at that.

Sometimes he carried Americans to look at villas for rent, and when the front glass of the automobile was up, curious fragments of conversation drifted out to him from within.

'…heard this fellow was a Russian prince…' 'Sh!…' 'No, this one right here…' 'Be quiet, Esther!' – followed by subdued laughter.

When the car stopped, his passengers would edge around to have a look at him. At first he was desperately unhappy when girls did this; after a while he didn't mind any more. Once a cheerfully intoxicated American asked him if it were true and invited him to lunch, and another time an elderly woman seized his hand as she got out of the taxi, shook it violently and then pressed a hundred-franc note into his hand.

'Well, Florence, now I can tell 'em back home I shook hands with a Russian prince.'

The inebriated American who had invited him to lunch thought at first that Val was a son of the Tsar, and it had to be explained to him that a prince in Russia was simply the equivalent of a British courtesy lord. But he was puzzled that a man of Val's personality didn't go out and make some real money.

'This is Europe,' said Val gravely. 'Here money is not made. It is inherited or else it is slowly saved over a period of many years and maybe in three generations a family moves up into a higher class.'

'Think of something people want – like we do.'

'That is because there is more money to want with in America. Everything that people want here has been thought of long ago.'

But after a year and with the help of a young Englishman he had played tennis with before the War, Val managed to get into the Cannes branch of an English bank. He forwarded mail and bought railroad tickets and arranged tours for impatient sightseers. Sometimes a familiar face came to his window; if Val was recognised he shook hands; if not he kept silence. After two years he was no longer pointed out as a former prince, for the Russians were an old story now – the splendour of the Rostovs and their friends was forgotten.

He mixed with people very little. In the evenings he walked for a while on the promenade, took a slow glass of beer in a café, and went early to bed. He was seldom invited anywhere because people thought that his sad, intent face was depressing – and he never accepted anyhow. He wore cheap French clothes now instead of the rich tweeds and flannels that had been ordered with his father's from England. As for women, he knew none at all. Of the many things he had been certain about at seventeen, he had been most certain about this – that his life would be full of romance. Now after eight years he knew that it was not to be. Somehow he had never had time for love – the War, the Revolution and now his poverty had conspired against his expectant heart. The springs of his emotion which had first poured forth one April night had dried up immediately and only a faint trickle remained.

His happy youth had ended almost before it began. He saw himself growing older and more shabby, and living always more and more in the memories of his gorgeous boyhood. Eventually he would become absurd, pulling out an old heirloom of a watch and showing it to amused young fellow-clerks who would listen with winks to his tales of the Rostov name.

He was thinking these gloomy thoughts one April evening in 1922 as he walked beside the sea and watched the never-changing magic of the awakening lights. It was no longer for his benefit, that magic, but it went on, and he was somehow glad. Tomorrow he was going away on his vacation, to a cheap hotel further down the shore where he could bathe and rest and read; then he would come back and work some more. Every year for three years he had taken his vacation during the last two weeks in April, perhaps because it was then that he felt the most need for remembering. It was in April that what was destined to be the best part of his life had come to a culmination under a romantic moonlight. It was sacred to him – for what he had thought of as an initiation and a beginning had turned out to be the end.

He paused now in front of the *Café des Etrangers* and after a moment crossed the street on impulse and sauntered down to the shore. A dozen yachts, already turned to a beautiful silver colour, rode at anchor in the bay. He had seen them that afternoon, and read the names painted on their bows – but only from habit. He had done it for three years now, and it was almost a natural function of his eye.

'*Un beau soir*,' remarked a French voice at his elbow. It was a boatman who had often seen Val here before. 'Monsieur finds the sea beautiful?'

'Very beautiful.'

'I too. But a bad living except in the season. Next week, though, I earn something special. I am paid well for simply waiting here and doing nothing more from eight o'clock until midnight.'

'That's very nice,' said Val politely.

'A widowed lady, very beautiful, from America, whose yacht always anchors in the harbour for the last two weeks in April. If the *Privateer* comes tomorrow it will make three years.'

5

All night Val didn't sleep – not because there was any question in his mind as to what he should do, but because his long stupefied emotions were suddenly awake and alive. Of course he must not see her – not he, a poor failure with a name that was now only a shadow – but it would make him a little happier always to know that she remembered. It gave his own memory another dimension, raised it like those stereopticon glasses that bring out a picture from the flat paper. It made him sure that he had not deceived himself – he had been charming once upon a time to a lovely woman, and she did not forget.

An hour before train time next day he was at the railway station with his grip, so as to avoid any chance encounter in the street. He found himself a place in a third-class carriage of the waiting train.

Somehow as he sat there he felt differently about life – a sort of hope, faint and illusory, that he hadn't felt twenty-four hours before. Perhaps there was some way in the next few years in which he could make it possible to meet her once again – if he worked hard, threw himself passionately into whatever was at hand. He knew of at least two Russians in Cannes who had started over again with nothing except good manners and ingenuity and were now doing surprisingly well. The blood of Morris Hasylton began to throb a little in Val's temples and made him remember something he had never before cared to remember – that Morris Hasylton, who had built his daughter a palace in St Petersburg, had also started from nothing at all.

Simultaneously another emotion possessed him, less strange, less dynamic but equally American – the emotion of curiosity. In case he did – well, in case life should ever make it possible for him to seek her out, he should at least know her name.

He jumped to his feet, fumbled excitedly at the carriage handle and jumped from the train. Tossing his valise into the checkroom he started at a run for the American consulate.

'A yacht came in this morning,' he said hurriedly to a clerk, 'an American yacht – the *Privateer*. I want to know who owns it.'

'Just a minute,' said the clerk, looking at him oddly. 'I'll try to find out.'

After what seemed to Val an interminable time he returned.

'Why, just a minute,' he repeated hesitantly. 'We're – it seems we're finding out.'

'Did the yacht come?'

'Oh, yes – it's here all right. At least I think so. If you'll just wait in that chair.'

After another ten minutes Val looked impatiently at his watch. If they didn't hurry he'd probably miss his train. He made a nervous movement as if to get up from his chair.

'Please sit still,' said the clerk, glancing at him quickly from his desk. 'I ask you. Just sit down in that chair.'

'I'll miss my train,' he said impatiently. 'I'm sorry to have given you all this bother –'

'Please sit still! We're glad to get it off our hands. You see, we've been waiting for your enquiry for – ah – three years.'

Val jumped to his feet and jammed his hat on his head.

'Why didn't you tell me that?' he demanded angrily.

'Because we had to get word to our – our client. Please don't go! It's – ah, it's too late.'

Val turned. Someone slim and radiant with dark frightened eyes was standing behind him, framed against the sunshine of the doorway.

'Why –'

Val's lips parted, but no words came through. She took a step towards him.

'I –' She looked at him helplessly, her eyes filling with tears. 'I just wanted to say hello,' she murmured. 'I've come back for three years just because I wanted to say hello.'

Still Val was silent.

'You might answer,' she said impatiently. 'You might answer when I'd – when I'd just about begun to think you'd been killed in the War.' She turned to the clerk. 'Please introduce us!' she cried. 'You see, I can't say hello to him when we don't even know each other's names.'

It's the thing to distrust these international marriages, of course. It's an American tradition that they always turn out badly, and we are accustomed to such headlines as: 'Would Trade Coronet for True American Love, Says Duchess', and 'Claims Count Mendicant Tortured Toledo Wife'. The other sort of headlines are never printed, for who would want to read: 'Castle is Love Nest, Asserts Former Georgia Belle', or 'Duke and Packer's Daughter Celebrate Golden Honeymoon'.

So far there have been no headlines at all about the young Rostovs. Prince Val is much too absorbed in that string of moonlight-blue taxicabs which he manipulates with such unusual efficiency, to give out interviews. He and his wife only leave New York once a year – but there is still a boatman who rejoices when the *Privateer* steams into Cannes harbour on a mid-April night.

The Swimmers

1

In the Place Benoît, a suspended mass of gasoline exhaust cooked slowly by the June sun. It was a terrible thing, for, unlike pure heat, it held no promise of rural escape, but suggested only roads choked with the same foul asthma. In the offices of the Promissory Trust Company, Paris Branch, facing the square, an American man of thirty-five inhaled it, and it became the odour of the thing he must presently do. A black horror suddenly descended upon him, and he went up to the washroom, where he stood, trembling a little, just inside the door.

Through the washroom window his eyes fell upon a sign – 1,000 'Chemises'. The shirts in question filled the shop window, piled, cravated and stuffed, or else draped with shoddy grace on the showcase floor. 1,000 'Chemises' – Count them! To the left he read 'Papeterie', 'Pâtisserie', 'Solde', 'Réclame', and Constance Talmadge in 'Déjeuner de Soleil'; and his eye, escaping to the right, met yet more sombre announcements: 'Vêtements Ecclésiastiques', 'Déclaration de Décès', and 'Pompes Funèbres'. Life and Death.

Henry Marston's trembling became a shaking; it would be pleasant if this were the end and nothing more need be done, he thought, and with a certain hope he sat down on a stool. But it is seldom really the end, and after a while, as he became too exhausted to care, the shaking stopped and he was better. Going downstairs, looking as alert and self-possessed as any other officer of the bank, he spoke to two clients he knew, and set his face grimly towards noon.

'Well, Henry Clay Marston!' A handsome old man shook hands with him and took the chair beside his desk.

'Henry, I want to see you in regard to what we talked about the other night. How about lunch? In that green little place with all the trees.'

'Not lunch, Judge Waterbury; I've got an engagement.'

'I'll talk now, then; because I'm leaving this afternoon. What do these plutocrats give you for looking important around here?'

Henry Marston knew what was coming.

'Ten thousand and certain expense money,' he answered.

'How would you like to come back to Richmond at about double that? You've been over here eight years and you don't know the opportunities you're missing. Why both my boys –'

Henry listened appreciatively, but this morning he couldn't concentrate on the matter. He spoke vaguely about being able to live more comfortably in Paris and restrained himself from stating his frank opinion upon existence at home.

Judge Waterbury beckoned to a tall, pale man who stood at the mail desk.

'This is Mr Wiese,' he said. 'Mr Wiese's from downstate; he's a halfway partner of mine.'

'Glad to meet you, suh.' Mr Wiese's voice was rather too deliberately Southern. 'Understand the judge is makin' you a proposition.'

'Yes,' Henry answered briefly. He recognised and detested the type – the prosperous sweater, presumably evolved from a cross between carpetbagger and poor White. When Wiese moved away, the judge said almost apologetically:

'He's one of the richest men in the South, Henry.' Then, after a pause: 'Come home, boy.'

'I'll think it over, Judge.' For a moment the grey and ruddy head seemed so kind; then it faded back into something one-dimensional, machine-finished, blandly and bleakly un-European. Henry Marston respected that open kindness – in the bank he touched it with daily appreciation, as a curator in a museum might touch a precious object removed in time and space, but there was no help in it for him; the questions which Henry Marston's life propounded could be answered only in France. His seven generations of Virginia ancestors were definitely behind him every day at noon when he returned home.

Home was a fine high-ceiling apartment hewn from the palace of a Renaissance cardinal in the rue Monsieur – the sort of thing Henry could not have afforded in America. Choupette, with something more than the rigid traditionalism of a French bourgeois taste, had made it beautiful, and moved through gracefully with their children. She was a frail Latin blonde with fine large features and vividly sad French eyes that had first fascinated Henry in a Grenoble *pension* in 1918. The two boys took their looks from Henry, voted the handsomest man at the University of Virginia a few years before the War.

Climbing the two broad flights of stairs, Henry stood panting a moment in the outside hall. It was quiet and cool here, and yet it was vaguely like the terrible thing that was going to happen. He heard a clock inside his apartment strike one, and inserted his key in the door.

The maid who had been in Choupette's family for thirty years stood before him, her mouth open in the utterance of a truncated sigh.

'*Bonjour,* Louise.'

'Monsieur!' He threw his hat on a chair. 'But, monsieur – but I thought monsieur said on the phone he was going to Tours for the children!'

'I changed my mind, Louise.'

He had taken a step forward, his last doubt melting away at the constricted terror in the woman's face.

'Is madame home?'

Simultaneously he perceived a man's hat and stick on the hall table and for the first time in his life he heard silence – a loud, singing silence, oppressive as heavy guns or thunder. Then, as the endless moment was broken by the maid's terrified little cry, he pushed through the *portières* into the next room.

An hour later Dr Derocco, *de la Faculté de Médecine,* rang the apartment bell. Choupette Marston, her face a little drawn and rigid, answered the door. For a moment they went through French forms; then:

'My husband has been feeling unwell for some weeks,' she said concisely. 'Nevertheless, he did not complain in a way to make me uneasy. He has suddenly collapsed; he cannot articulate or move his limbs. All this, I must say, might have been precipitated by a certain indiscretion of mine – in all events, there was a violent scene, a discussion, and sometimes, when he is agitated, my husband cannot comprehend well in French.'

'I will see him,' said the doctor, thinking: 'Some things are comprehended instantly in all languages.'

During the next four weeks several people listened to strange speeches about one thousand chemises, and heard how all the population of Paris was becoming etherised by cheap gasoline – there was a consulting psychiatrist, not inclined to believe in any underlying mental trouble; there was a nurse from the American Hospital, and there was Choupette, frightened, defiant and, after her fashion, deeply sorry. A month later, when Henry awoke to his familiar room, lit with a dimmed lamp, he found her sitting beside his bed and reached out for her hand.

'I still love you,' he said – 'that's the odd thing.'

'Sleep, male cabbage.'

'At all costs,' he continued with a certain feeble irony, 'you can count on me to adopt the Continental attitude.'

'Please! You tear at my heart.'

When he was sitting up in bed they were ostensibly close together again – closer than they had been for months.

'Now you're going to have another holiday,' said Henry to the two boys, back from the country. 'Papa has got to go to the seashore and get really well.'

'Will we swim?'

'And get drowned, my darlings?' Choupette cried. 'But fancy, at your age. Not at all!'

So, at St Jean de Luz they sat on the shore instead, and watched the English and Americans and a few hardy French pioneers of *le sport* voyage between raft and diving tower, motor boat and sand. There were passing ships, and bright islands to look at, and mountains reaching into cold zones, and red and yellow villas, called *Fleur des Bois*, *Mon Hid*, or *Sans-Souci*; and further back, tired French villages of baked cement and grey stone.

Choupette sat at Henry's side, holding a parasol to shelter her peach-bloom skin from the sun.

'Look!' she would say, at the sight of tanned American girls. 'Is that lovely? Skin that will be leather at thirty – a sort of brown veil to hide all blemishes, so that everyone will look alike. And women of a hundred kilos in such bathing suits! Weren't clothes intended to hide Nature's mistakes?'

Henry Clay Marston was a Virginian of the kind who are prouder of being Virginians than of being Americans. That mighty word printed across a continent was less to him than the memory of his grandfather, who freed his slaves in '58[7], fought from Manassas to Appomattox[8],

74

knew Huxley and Spencer[9] as light reading, and believed in caste only when it expressed the best of race.

To Choupette all this was vague. Her more specific criticisms of his compatriots were directed against the women.

'How would you place them?' she exclaimed. 'Great ladies, bourgeoises, adventuresses, they are all the same. Look! Where would I be if I tried to act like your friend, Madame de Richepin? My father was a professor in a provincial university, and I have certain things I wouldn't do because they wouldn't please my class, my family. Madame de Richepin has other things she wouldn't do because of her class, her family.' Suddenly she pointed to an American girl going into the water: 'But that young lady may be a stenographer and yet be compelled to warp herself, dressing and acting as if she had all the money in the world.'

'Perhaps she will have, some day.'

'That's the story they are told; it happens to one, not to the ninety-nine. That's why all their faces over thirty are discontented and un-happy.'

Though Henry was in general agreement, he could not help being amused at Choupette's choice of target this afternoon. The girl – she was perhaps eighteen – was obviously acting like nothing but herself – she was what his father would have called a thoroughbred. A deep, thoughtful face that was pretty only because of the irrepressible determination of the perfect features to be recognised, a face that could have done without them and not yielded up its poise and distinction.

In her grace, at once exquisite and hardy, she was that perfect type of American girl that makes one wonder if the male is not being sacrificed to it, much as, in the last century, the lower strata in England were sacrificed to produce the governing class.

The two young men, coming out of the water as she went in, had large shoulders and empty faces. She had a smile for them that was no more than they deserved – that must do until she chose one to be the father of her children and gave herself up to destiny. Until then – Henry Marston was glad about her as her arms, like flying fish, clipped the water in a crawl, as her body spread in a swan dive or doubled in a

75

jackknife from the springboard and her head appeared from the depth, jauntily flipping the damp hair away.

The two young men passed near.

'They push water,' Choupette said, 'then they go elsewhere and push other water. They pass months in France and they couldn't tell you the name of the President. They are parasites such as Europe has not known in a hundred years.'

But Henry had stood up abruptly, and now all the people on the beach were suddenly standing up. Something had happened out there in the fifty yards between the deserted raft and the shore. The bright head showed upon the surface; it did not flip water now, but called: '*Au secours!* Help!' in a feeble and frightened voice.

'Henry!' Choupette cried. 'Stop! Henry!'

The beach was almost deserted at noon, but Henry and several others were sprinting towards the sea; the two young Americans heard, turned and sprinted after them. There was a frantic little time with half a dozen bobbing heads in the water. Choupette, still clinging to her parasol, but managing to wring her hands at the same time, ran up and down the beach crying: 'Henry! Henry!'

Now there were more helping hands, and then two swelling groups around prostrate figures on the shore. The young fellow who pulled in the girl brought her around in a minute or so, but they had more trouble getting the water out of Henry, who had never learnt to swim.

2

'This is the man who didn't know whether he could swim, because he'd never tried.'

Henry got up from his sun chair, grinning. It was next morning, and the saved girl had just appeared on the beach with her brother. She smiled back at Henry, brightly casual, appreciative rather than grateful.

'At the very least, I owe it to you to teach you how,' she said.

'I'd like it. I decided that in the water yesterday, just before I went down the tenth time.'

'You can trust me. I'll never again eat chocolate ice cream before going in.'

As she went on into the water, Choupette asked: 'How long do you think we'll stay here? After all, this life wearies one.'

'We'll stay till I can swim. And the boys too.'

'Very well. I saw a nice bathing suit in two shades of blue for fifty francs that I will buy you this afternoon.'

Feeling a little paunchy and unhealthily white, Henry, holding his sons by the hand, took his body into the water. The breakers leapt at him, staggering him, while the boys yelled with ecstasy; the returning water curled threateningly around his feet as it hurried back to sea. Further out, he stood waist-deep with other intimidated souls, watching the people dive from the raft tower, hoping the girl would come to fulfill her promise, and somewhat embarrassed when she did.

'I'll start with your eldest. You watch and then try it by yourself.'

He floundered in the water. It went into his nose and started a raw stinging; it blinded him; it lingered afterwards in his ears, rattling back and forth like pebbles for hours. The sun discovered him, too, peeling long strips of parchment from his shoulders, blistering his back so that he lay in a feverish agony for several nights. After a week he swam, painfully, pantingly, and not very far. The girl taught him a sort of crawl, for he saw that the breast stroke was an obsolete device that lingered on with the inept and the old. Choupette caught him regarding his tanned face in the mirror with a sort of fascination, and the youngest boy contracted some sort of mild skin infection in the sand that retired him from competition. But one day Henry battled his way desperately to the float and drew himself up on it with his last breath.

'That being settled,' he told the girl, when he could speak, 'I can leave for St Jean tomorrow.'

'I'm sorry.'

'What will you do now?'

'My brother and I are going to Antibes; there's swimming there all through October. Then Florida.'

'And swim?' he asked with some amusement.

'Why, yes. We'll swim.'

'Why do you swim?'

'To get clean,' she answered surprisingly.

'Clean from what?'

She frowned. 'I don't know why I said that. But it feels clean in the sea.'

'Americans are too particular about that,' he commented.

'How could anyone be?'

'I mean we've got too fastidious even to clean up our messes.'

'I don't know.'

'But tell me why you –' He stopped himself in surprise. He had been about to ask her to explain a lot of things – to say what was clean and unclean, what was worth knowing and what was only words – to open up a new gate to life. Looking for a last time into her eyes, full of cool secrets, he realised how much he was going to miss these mornings, without knowing whether it was the girl who interested him or what she represented of his ever-new, ever-changing country.

'All right,' he told Choupette that night. 'We'll leave tomorrow.'

'For Paris?'

'For America.'

'You mean I'm to go too? And the children?'

'Yes.'

'But that's absurd,' she protested. 'Last time it cost more than we spend in six months here. And then there were only three of us. Now that we've managed to get ahead at last –'

'That's just it. I'm tired of getting ahead on your skimping and saving and going without dresses. I've got to make more money. American men are incomplete without money.'

'You mean we'll stay?'

'It's very possible.'

They looked at each other and, against her will, Choupette understood. For eight years, by a process of ceaseless adaptation, he had lived her life, substituting for the moral confusion of his own country, the tradition, the wisdom, the sophistication of France. After that matter in Paris, it had seemed the bigger part to understand and to forgive, to cling to the home as something apart from the vagaries of love. Only now, glowing with a good health that he had not experienced for years, did he discover his true reaction. It had released him. For all his sense of loss, he possessed again the masculine self he had handed over to the keeping of a wise little Provençal girl eight years ago.

She struggled for a moment.

'You've got a good position and we really have plenty of money. You know we can live cheaper here.'

'The boys are growing up now, and I'm not sure I want to educate them in France.'

'But that's all decided,' she wailed. 'You admit yourself that education in America is superficial and full of silly fads. Do you want them to be like those two dummies on the beach?'

'Perhaps I was thinking more of myself, Choupette. Men just out of college who brought their letters of credit into the bank eight years ago, travel about with ten-thousand-dollar cars now. I didn't use to care. I used to tell myself that I had a better place to escape to, just because we knew that lobster armoricaine was really lobster américaine[10]. Perhaps I haven't that feeling any more.'

She stiffened. 'If that's it –'

'It's up to you. We'll make a new start.'

Choupette thought for a moment. 'Of course my sister can take over the apartment.'

'Of course.' He waxed enthusiastic. 'And there are sure to be things that'll tickle you – we'll have a nice car, for instance, and one of those electric iceboxes, and all sorts of funny machines to take the place of servants. It won't be bad. You'll learn to play golf and talk about children all day. Then there are the movies.'

Choupette groaned.

'It's going to be pretty awful at first,' he admitted, 'but there are still a few good nigger cooks, and we'll probably have two bathrooms.'

'I am unable to use more than one at a time.'

'You'll learn.'

A month afterwards, when the beautiful white island floated towards them in the Narrows, Henry's throat grew constricted with the rest and he wanted to cry out to Choupette and all foreigners, 'Now, you see!'

Almost three years later, Henry Marston walked out of his office in the Calumet Tobacco Company and along the hall to Judge Waterbury's suite. His face was older, with a suspicion of grimness, and a slight irrepressible heaviness of body was not concealed by his white linen suit.

'Busy, Judge?'

'Come in, Henry.'

'I'm going to the shore tomorrow to swim off this weight. I wanted to talk to you before I go.'

'Children going too?'

'Oh, sure.'

'Choupette'll go abroad, I suppose.'

'Not this year. I think she's coming with me, if she doesn't stay here in Richmond.'

The judge thought: 'There isn't a doubt but what he knows everything.' He waited.

'I wanted to tell you, Judge, that I'm resigning the end of September.'

The judge's chair creaked backwards as he brought his feet to the floor.

'You're quitting, Henry?'

'Not exactly. Walter Ross wants to come home; let me take his place in France.'

'Boy, do you know what we pay Walter Ross?'

'Seven thousand.'

'And you're getting twenty-five.'

'You've probably heard I've made something in the market,' said Henry deprecatingly.

'I've heard everything between a hundred thousand and half a million.'

'Somewhere in between.'

'Then why a seven-thousand-dollar job? Is Choupette homesick?'

'No, I think Choupette likes it over here. She's adapted herself amazingly.'

'He knows,' the judge thought. 'He wants to get away.'

After Henry had gone, he looked up at the portrait of his grandfather on the wall. In those days the matter would have been simpler. Duelling pistols in the old Wharton meadow at dawn. It would be to Henry's advantage if things were like that today.

Henry's chauffeur dropped him in front of a Georgian house in a new suburban section. Leaving his hat in the hall, he went directly out on the side veranda.

From the swaying canvas swing Choupette looked up with a polite smile. Save for a certain alertness of feature and a certain indefinable knack of putting things on, she might have passed for an American. Southernisms overlay her French accent with a quaint charm; there were still college boys who rushed her like a debutante at the Christmas dances.

Henry nodded at Mr Charles Wiese, who occupied a wicker chair, with a gin fizz at his elbow.

'I want to talk to you,' he said, sitting down.

Wiese's glance and Choupette's crossed quickly before coming to rest on him.

'You're free, Wiese,' Henry said. 'Why don't you and Choupette get married?'

Choupette sat up, eyes flashing.

'Now wait.' Henry turned back to Wiese. 'I've been letting this thing drift for about a year now, while I got my financial affairs in shape. But this last brilliant idea of yours makes me feel a little uncomfortable, a little sordid, and I don't want to feel that way.'

'Just what do you mean?' Wiese enquired.

'On my last trip to New York you had me shadowed. I presume it was with the intention of getting divorce evidence against me. It wasn't a success.'

'I don't know where you got such an idea in your head, Marston; you –'

'Don't lie!'

'Suh –' Wiese began, but Henry interrupted impatiently:

'Now don't "Suh" me, and don't try to whip yourself up into a temper. You're not talking to a scared picker full of hookworm. I don't want a scene; my emotions aren't sufficiently involved. I want to arrange a divorce.'

'Why do you bring it up like this?' Choupette cried, breaking into French. 'Couldn't we talk of it alone, if you think you have so much against me?'

'Wait a minute; this might as well be settled now,' Wiese said. 'Choupette does want a divorce. Her life with you is unsatisfactory, and the only reason she has kept on is because she's an idealist. You don't seem to appreciate that fact, but it's true; she couldn't bring herself to break up her home.'

'Very touching.' Henry looked at Choupette with bitter amusement. 'But let's come down to facts. I'd like to close up this matter before I go back to France.'

Again Wiese and Choupette exchanged a look.

'It ought to be simple,' Wiese said. 'Choupette doesn't want a cent of your money.'

'I know. What she wants is the children. The answer is, you can't have the children.'

'How perfectly outrageous!' Choupette cried. 'Do you imagine for a minute I'm going to give up my children?'

'What's your idea, Marston?' demanded Wiese. 'To take them back to France and make them expatriates like yourself?'

'Hardly that. They're entered for St Regis School and then for Yale. And I haven't any idea of not letting them see their mother whenever she so desires – judging from the past two years, it won't be often. But I intend to have their entire legal custody.'

'Why?' they demanded together.

'Because of the home.'

'What the devil do you mean?'

'I'd rather apprentice them to a trade than have them brought up in the sort of home yours and Choupette's is going to be.'

There was a moment's silence. Suddenly Choupette picked up her glass, dashed the contents at Henry and collapsed on the settee, passionately sobbing.

Henry dabbed his face with his handkerchief and stood up.

'I was afraid of that,' he said, 'but I think I've made my position clear.'

He went up to his room and lay down on the bed. In a thousand wakeful hours during the past year he had fought over in his mind the problem of keeping his boys without taking those legal measures against Choupette that he could not bring himself to take. He knew that she wanted the children only because without them she would be suspect, even *déclassée*, to her family in France; but with that quality of detachment peculiar to old stock, Henry recognised this as a perfectly legitimate motive. Furthermore, no public scandal must touch the mother of his sons – it was this that had rendered his challenge so ineffectual this afternoon.

When difficulties became insurmountable, inevitable, Henry sought surcease in exercise. For three years, swimming had been a sort of refuge, and he turned to it as one man to music or another to drink. There was a point when he would resolutely stop thinking and go to the Virginia coast for a week to wash his mind in water. Far out past the breakers he could survey the green-and-brown line of the Old Dominion with the pleasant impersonality of a porpoise. The burden of his wretched marriage fell away with the buoyant tumble of his body among the swells, and he would begin to move in a child's dream of space. Sometimes remembered playmates of his youth swam with him; sometimes, with his two sons beside him, he seemed to be setting off along the bright pathway to the moon. Americans, he liked to say, should be born with fins, and perhaps they were – perhaps money was a form of fin. In England property begot a strong place sense, but Americans, restless and with shallow roots, needed fins and wings. There was even a recurrent idea in America about an education that would leave out history and the past, that should be a sort of equipment for aerial adventure, weighed down by none of the stowaways of inheritance or tradition.

Thinking of this in the water the next afternoon brought Henry's mind to the children; he turned and at a slow trudgen started back towards the shore. Out of condition, he rested, panting, at the raft, and glancing up, he saw familiar eyes. In a moment he was talking with the girl he had tried to rescue four years ago.

He was overjoyed. He had not realised how vividly he remembered her. She was a Virginian – he might have guessed it abroad – the laziness, the apparent casualness that masked an unfailing courtesy and attention; a good form devoid of forms was based on kindness and consideration. Hearing her name for the first time, he recognised it – an Eastern-shore name, 'good' as his own.

Lying in the sun, they talked like old friends, not about races and manners and the things that Henry brooded over Choupette, but rather as if they naturally agreed about those things; they talked about what they liked themselves and about what was fun. She showed him a sitting-down, standing-up dive from the high springboard, and he emulated her inexpertly – that was fun. They talked about eating soft-shelled crabs, and she told him how, because of the curious acoustics of the water, one could lie there and be diverted by conversations on the hotel porch. They tried it and heard two ladies over their tea say:

'Now, at the Lido –'

'Now, at Asbury Park –'

'Oh, my dear, he just scratched and scratched all night; he just scratched and scratched –'

'My dear, at Deauville –'

'– scratched and scratched all night.'

After a while the sea got to be that very blue colour of four o'clock, and the girl told him how, at nineteen, she had been divorced from a Spaniard who locked her in the hotel suite when he went out at night.

'It was one of those things,' she said lightly. 'But speaking more cheerfully, how's your beautiful wife? And the boys – did they learn to float? Why can't you all dine with me tonight?'

'I'm afraid I won't be able to,' he said, after a moment's hesitation. He must do nothing, however trivial, to furnish Choupette weapons, and with a feeling of disgust, it occurred to him that he was possibly being watched this afternoon. Nevertheless, he was glad of his caution when she unexpectedly arrived at the hotel for dinner that night.

After the boys had gone to bed, they faced each other over coffee on the hotel veranda.

'Will you kindly explain why I'm not entitled to a half share in my own children?' Choupette began. 'It is not like you to be vindictive, Henry.'

It was hard for Henry to explain. He told her again that she could have the children when she wanted them, but that he must exercise entire control over them because of certain old-fashioned convictions –

watching her face grow harder, minute by minute, he saw there was no use, and broke off. She made a scornful sound.

'I wanted to give you a chance to be reasonable before Charles arrives.'

Henry sat up. 'Is he coming here this evening?'

'Happily. And I think perhaps your selfishness is going to have a jolt, Henry. You're not dealing with a woman now.'

When Wiese walked out on the porch an hour later, Henry saw that his pale lips were like chalk; there was a deep flush on his forehead and hard confidence in his eyes. He was cleared for action and he wasted no time. 'We've got something to say to each other, suh, and since I've got a motor boat here, perhaps that'd be the quietest place to say it.'

Henry nodded coolly; five minutes later the three of them were headed out into Hampton Roads on the wide fairway of the moonlight. It was a tranquil evening, and half a mile from shore Wiese cut down the engine to a mild throbbing, so that they seemed to drift without will or direction through the bright water. His voice broke the stillness abruptly:

'Marston, I'm going to talk to you straight from the shoulder. I love Choupette and I'm not apologising for it. These things have happened before in this world. I guess you understand that. The only difficulty is this matter of the custody of Choupette's children. You seem determined to try and take them away from the mother that bore them and raised them' – Wiese's words became more clearly articulated, as if they came from a wider mouth – 'but you left one thing out of your calculations, and that's me. Do you happen to realise that at this moment I'm one of the richest men in Virginia?'

'I've heard as much.'

'Well, money is power, Marston. I repeat, suh, money is power.'

'I've heard that too. In fact, you're a bore, Wiese.' Even by the moon Henry could see the crimson deepen on his brow.

'You'll hear it again, suh. Yesterday you took us by surprise and I was unprepared for your brutality to Choupette. But this morning I received a letter from Paris that puts the matter in a new light. It is a statement by a specialist in mental diseases, declaring you to be of unsound mind, and unfit to have the custody of children. The specialist is the one who attended you in your nervous breakdown four years ago.'

Henry laughed incredulously, and looked at Choupette, half expecting her to laugh, too, but she had turned her face away, breathing quickly through parted lips. Suddenly he realised that Wiese was telling the truth – that by some extraordinary bribe he had obtained such a document and fully intended to use it.

For a moment Henry reeled as if from a material blow. He listened to his own voice saying, 'That's the most ridiculous thing I ever heard,' and to Wiese's answer: 'They don't always tell people when they have mental troubles.'

Suddenly Henry wanted to laugh, and the terrible instant when he had wondered if there could be some shred of truth in the allegation passed. He turned to Choupette, but again she avoided his eyes.

'How could you, Choupette?'

'I want my children,' she began, but Wiese broke in quickly:

'If you'd been halfway fair, Marston, we wouldn't have resorted to this step.'

'Are you trying to pretend you arranged this scurvy trick since yesterday afternoon?'

'I believe in being prepared, but if you had been reasonable – in fact, if you will be reasonable – this opinion needn't be used.' His voice became paternal, almost kind: 'Be wise, Marston. On your side there's an obstinate prejudice; on mine there are forty million dollars. Don't fool yourself. Let me repeat, Marston, that money is power. You were abroad so long that perhaps you're inclined to forget that fact. Money made this country, built its great and glorious cities, created its industries, covered it with an iron network of railroads. It's money that harnesses the forces of Nature, creates the machine and makes it go when money says go, and stop when money says stop.'

As though interpreting this as a command, the engine gave forth a sudden hoarse sound and came to rest.

'What is it?' demanded Choupette.

'It's nothing.' Wiese pressed the self-starter with his foot. 'I repeat, Marston, that money – The battery is dry. One minute while I spin the wheel.'

He spun it for the best part of fifteen minutes while the boat meandered about in a placid little circle.

'Choupette, open that drawer behind you and see if there isn't a rocket.'

A touch of panic had crept into her voice when she answered that there was no rocket. Wiese eyed the shore tentatively.

'There's no use in yelling; we must be half a mile out. We'll just have to wait here until someone comes along.'

'We won't wait here,' Henry remarked.

'Why not?'

'We're moving towards the bay. Can't you tell? We're moving out with the tide.'

'That's impossible!' said Choupette sharply.

'Look at those two lights on shore – one passing the other now. Do you see?'

'Do something!' she wailed, and then, in a burst of French: *'Ah, c'est épouvantable! N'est-ce pas qu'il y a quelque chose qu'on peut faire?'*[11]

The tide was running fast now, and the boat was drifting down the Roads with it towards the sea. The vague blots of two ships passed them, but at a distance, and there was no answer to their hail. Against the western sky a lighthouse blinked, but it was impossible to guess how near to it they would pass.

'It looks as if all our difficulties would be solved for us,' Henry said.

'What difficulties?' Choupette demanded. 'Do you mean there's nothing to be done? Can you sit there and just float away like this?'

'It may be easier on the children, after all.' He winced as Choupette began to sob bitterly, but he said nothing. A ghostly idea was taking shape in his mind.

'Look here, Marston. Can you swim?' demanded Wiese, frowning.

'Yes, but Choupette can't.'

'I can't either – I didn't mean that. If you could swim in and get to a telephone, the coastguard people would send for us.'

Henry surveyed the dark, receding shore.

'It's too far,' he said.

'You can try!' said Choupette.

Henry shook his head.

87

'Too risky. Besides, there's an outside chance that we'll be picked up.'

The lighthouse passed them, far to the left and out of earshot. Another one, the last, loomed up half a mile away.

'We might drift to France like that man Gerbault[12],' Henry remarked. 'But then, of course, we'd be expatriates – and Wiese wouldn't like that, would you, Wiese?'

Wiese, fussing frantically with the engine, looked up.

'See what you can do with this,' he said.

'I don't know anything about mechanics,' Henry answered. 'Besides, this solution of our difficulties grows on me. Just suppose you were dirty dog enough to use that statement and got the children because of it – in that case I wouldn't have much impetus to go on living. We're all failures – I as head of my household, Choupette as a wife and a mother, and you, Wiese, as a human being. It's just as well that we go out of life together.'

'This is no time for a speech, Marston.'

'Oh yes, it's a fine time. How about a little more house-organ oratory about money being power?'

Choupette sat rigid in the bow; Wiese stood over the engine, biting nervously at his lips.

'We're not going to pass that lighthouse very close.' An idea suddenly occurred to him. 'Couldn't you swim to that, Marston?'

'Of course he could!' Choupette cried.

Henry looked at it tentatively.

'I might. But I won't.'

'You've got to!'

Again he flinched at Choupette's weeping; simultaneously he saw the time had come.

'Everything depends on one small point,' he said rapidly. 'Wiese, have you got a fountain pen?'

'Yes. What for?'

'If you'll write and sign about two hundred words at my dictation, I'll swim to the lighthouse and get help. Otherwise, so help me God, we'll drift out to sea! And you better decide in about one minute.'

'Oh, anything!' Choupette broke out frantically. 'Do what he says,

88

Charles; he means it. He always means what he says. Oh, please don't wait!'

'I'll do what you want' – Wiese's voice was shaking – 'only, for God's sake, go on. What is it you want – an agreement about the children? I'll give you my personal word of honour –'

'There's no time for humour,' said Henry savagely. 'Take this piece of paper and write.'

The two pages that Wiese wrote at Henry's dictation relinquished all lien on the children thence and for ever for himself and Choupette. When they had affixed trembling signatures Wiese cried:

'Now go, for God's sake, before it's too late!'

'Just one thing more: the certificate from the doctor.'

'I haven't it here.'

'You lie.'

Wiese took it from his pocket.

'Write across the bottom that you paid so much for it, and sign your name to that.'

A minute later, stripped to his underwear, and with the papers in an oiled-silk tobacco pouch suspended from his neck, Henry dived from the side of the boat and struck out towards the light.

The waters leapt up at him for an instant, but after the first shock it was all warm and friendly, and the small murmur of the waves was an encouragement. It was the longest swim he had ever tried, and he was straight from the city, but the happiness in his heart buoyed him up. Safe now, and free. Each stroke was stronger for knowing that his two sons, sleeping back in the hotel, were safe from what he dreaded. Divorced from her own country, Choupette had picked the things out of American life that pandered best to her own self-indulgence. That, backed by a court decree, she should be permitted to hand on this preposterous moral farrago to his sons was unendurable. He would have lost them for ever.

Turning on his back, he saw that already the motor boat was far away, the blinding light was nearer. He was very tired. If one let go – and, in the relaxation from strain, he felt an alarming impulse to let go – one died very quickly and painlessly, and all these problems of hate and bitterness disappeared. But he felt the fate of his sons in the oiled-silk pouch about his neck, and with a convulsive effort he turned over again and concentrated his energies on his goal.

Twenty minutes later he stood shivering and dripping in the signal room while it was broadcast out to the coast patrol that a launch was drifting in the bay.

'There's not much danger without a storm,' the keeper said. 'By now they've probably struck a cross-current from the river and drifted into Peyton Harbour.'

'Yes,' said Henry, who had come to this coast for three summers. 'I knew that too.'

4

In October, Henry left his sons in school and embarked on the *Majestic* for Europe. He had come home as to a generous mother and had been profusely given more than he asked – money, release from an intolerable situation, and the fresh strength to fight for his own. Watching the fading city, the fading shore, from the deck of the *Majestic*, he had a sense of overwhelming gratitude and gladness that America was there, that under the ugly debris of industry the rich land still pushed up, incorrigibly lavish and fertile, and that in the heart of the leaderless people the old generosities and devotions fought on, breaking out sometimes in fanaticism and excess, but indomitable and undefeated. There was a lost generation in the saddle at the moment, but it seemed to him that the men coming on, the men of the war, were better; and all his own feeling that America was a bizarre accident, a sort of historical sport, had gone for ever. The best of America was the best of the world.

Going down to the purser's office, he waited until a fellow-passenger was through at the window. When she turned, they both started, and he saw it was the girl.

'Oh, hello!' she cried. 'I'm glad you're going! I was just asking when the pool opened. The great thing about this ship is that you can always get a swim.'

'Why do you like to swim?' he demanded.

'You always ask me that.' She laughed.

'Perhaps you'll tell me if we had dinner together tonight.'

But when, in a moment, he left her he knew that she could never tell him – she or another. France was a land, England was a people, but America, having about it still that quality of the idea, was harder to utter – it was the graves at Shiloh and the tired, drawn, nervous faces of its great men, and the country boys dying in the Argonne for a phrase that was empty before their bodies withered. It was a willingness of the heart.

A New Leaf

1

It was the first day warm enough to eat outdoors in the Bois de Boulogne, while chestnut blossoms slanted down across the tables and dropped impudently into the butter and the wine. Julia Ross ate a few with her bread and listened to the big goldfish rippling in the pool and the sparrows whirring about an abandoned table. You could see everybody again – the waiters with their professional faces, the watchful Frenchwomen all heels and eyes, Phil Hoffman opposite her with his heart balanced on his fork, and the extraordinarily handsome man just coming out on the terrace.

> *... The purple noon's transparent might,*
> *The breath of the moist air is light,*
> *Around each unexpanded bud...*[13]

Julia trembled discreetly; she controlled herself; she didn't spring up and call, 'Yi-yi-yi-yi! Isn't this grand?' and push the maître d'hôtel into the lily pond. She sat there, a well-behaved woman of twenty-one, and discreetly trembled.

Phil was rising, napkin in hand. 'Hi there, Dick!'

'Hi, Phil!'

It was the handsome man; Phil took a few steps forward and they talked apart from the table.

' ... seen Carter and Kitty in Spain –'

' ... poured out on to the Bremen –'

' ... so I was going to –'

The man went on, following the head waiter, and Phil sat down.

'Who is that?' she demanded.

'A friend of mine – Dick Ragland.'

'He's without doubt the handsomest man I ever saw in my life.'

'Yes, he's handsome,' he agreed without enthusiasm.

'Handsome! He's an archangel, he's a mountain lion, he's something to eat. Just why didn't you introduce him?'

'Because he's got the worst reputation of any American in Paris.'

'Nonsense; he must be maligned. It's all a dirty frame-up – a lot of

95

jealous husbands whose wives got one look at him. Why, that man's never done anything in his life except lead cavalry charges and save children from drowning.'

'The fact remains he's not received anywhere – not for one reason but for a thousand.'

'What reasons?'

'Everything. Drink, women, jails, scandals, killed somebody with an automobile, lazy, worthless –'

'I don't believe a word of it,' said Julia firmly. 'I bet he's tremendously attractive. And you spoke to him as if you thought so too.'

'Yes,' he said reluctantly, 'like so many alcoholics, he has a certain charm. If he'd only make his messes off by himself somewhere – except right in people's laps. Just when somebody's taken him up and is making a big fuss over him, he pours the soup down the hostess' back, kisses the serving maid, and passes out in the dog kennel. But he's done it too often. He's run through about everybody, until there's no one left.'

'There's me,' said Julia.

There was Julia, who was a little too good for anybody and sometimes regretted that she had been so well endowed. Anything added to beauty has to be paid for – that is to say, the qualities that pass as substitutes can be liabilities when added to beauty itself. Julia's brilliant hazel glance was enough, without the questioning light of intelligence that flickered in it; her irrepressible sense of the ridiculous detracted from the gentle relief of her mouth, and the loveliness of her figure might have been more obvious if she had slouched and postured rather than sat and stood very straight, after the discipline of a strict father.

Equally perfect young men had several times appeared bearing gifts, but generally with the air of being already complete, of having no space for development. On the other hand, she found that men of a larger scale had sharp corners and edges in youth, and she was a little too young herself to like that. There was, for instance, this scornful young egotist, Phil Hoffman, opposite her, who was obviously going to be a brilliant lawyer and who had practically followed her to Paris. She liked him as well as anyone she knew, but he had at present all the overbearance of the son of a chief of police.

'Tonight I'm going to London, and Wednesday I sail,' he said. 'And you'll be in Europe all summer, with somebody new chewing on your ear every few weeks.'

'When you've been called for a lot of remarks like that you'll begin to edge into the picture,' Julia remarked. 'Just to square yourself, I want you to introduce that man Ragland.'

'My last few hours!' he complained.

'But I've given you three whole days on the chance you'd work out a better approach. Be a little civilised and ask him to have some coffee.'

As Mr Dick Ragland joined them, Julia drew a little breath of pleasure. He was a fine figure of a man, in colouring both tan and blond, with a peculiar luminosity to his face. His voice was quietly intense; it seemed always to tremble a little with a sort of gay despair; the way he looked at Julia made her feel attractive. For half an hour, as their sentences floated pleasantly among the scent of violets and snowdrops, forget-me-nots and pansies, her interest in him grew. She was even glad when Phil said:

'I've just thought about my English visa. I'll have to leave you two incipient lovebirds together against my better judgement. Will you meet me at the Gare St Lazare at five and see me off?'

He looked at Julia hoping she'd say, 'I'll go along with you now.' She knew very well she had no business being alone with this man, but he made her laugh, and she hadn't laughed much lately, so she said: 'I'll stay a few minutes; it's so nice and springy here.'

When Phil was gone, Dick Ragland suggested a *fine champagne*.

'I hear you have a terrible reputation?' she said impulsively.

'Awful. I'm not even invited out any more. Do you want me to slip on my false moustache?'

'It's so odd,' she pursued. 'Don't you cut yourself off from all nourishment? Do you know that Phil felt he had to warn me about you before he introduced you? And I might very well have told him not to.'

'Why didn't you?'

'I thought you seemed so attractive and it was such a pity.'

His face grew bland; Julia saw that the remark had been made so often that it no longer reached him.

'It's none of my business,' she said quickly. She did not realise that

97

his being a sort of outcast added to his attraction for her – not the dissipation itself, for never having seen it, it was merely an abstraction – but its result in making him so alone. Something atavistic in her went out to the stranger to the tribe, a being from a world with different habits from hers, who promised the unexpected – promised adventure.

'I'll tell you something else,' he said suddenly. 'I'm going permanently on the wagon from 5th June, my twenty-eighth birthday. I don't have fun drinking any more. Evidently I'm not one of the few people who can use liquor.'

'You sure you can go on the wagon?'

'I always do what I say I'll do. Also I'm going back to New York to go to work.'

'I'm really surprised how glad I am.' This was rash, but she let it stand.

'Have another *fine*?' Dick suggested. 'Then you'll be gladder still.'

'Will you go on this way right up to your birthday?'

'Probably. On my birthday I'll be on the *Olympic* in mid-ocean.'

'I'll be on that boat too!' she exclaimed.

'You can watch the quick change; I'll do it for the ship's concert.'

The tables were being cleared off. Julia knew she should go now, but she couldn't bear to leave him sitting with that unhappy look under his smile. She felt, maternally, that she ought to say something to help him keep his resolution.

'Tell me why you drink so much. Probably some obscure reason you don't know yourself.'

'Oh, I know pretty well how it began.'

He told her as another hour waned. He had gone to the war at seventeen and, when he came back, life as a Princeton freshman with a little black cap was somewhat tame. So he went up to Boston Tech and then abroad to the Beaux Arts; it was there that something happened to him.

'About the time I came into some money I found that with a few drinks I got expansive and somehow had the ability to please people, and the idea turned my head. Then I began to take a whole lot of drinks to keep going and have everybody think I was wonderful. Well,

I got plastered a lot and quarrelled with most of my friends, and then I met a wild bunch and for a while I was expansive with them. But I was inclined to get superior and suddenly think, "What am I doing with this bunch?" They didn't like that much. And when a taxi that I was in killed a man, I was sued. It was just a graft, but it got in the papers, and after I was released the impression remained that I'd killed him. So all I've got to show for the last few years is a reputation that makes mothers rush their daughters away if I'm at the same hotel.'

An impatient waiter was hovering near and she looked at her watch.

'Gosh, we're to see Phil off at five. We've been here all the afternoon.'

As they hurried to the Gare St Lazare, he asked: 'Will you let me see you again; or do you think you'd better not?'

She returned his long look. There was no sign of dissipation in his face, in his warm cheeks, in his erect carriage.

'I'm always fine at lunch,' he added, like an invalid.

'I'm not worried,' she laughed. 'Take me to lunch day after to-morrow.'

They hurried up the steps of the Gare St Lazare, only to see the last carriage of the Golden Arrow disappearing towards the Channel. Julia was remorseful because Phil had come so far.

As a sort of atonement, she went to the apartment where she lived with her aunt and tried to write a letter to him, but Dick Ragland intruded himself into her thoughts. By morning the effect of his good looks had faded a little; she was inclined to write him a note that she couldn't see him. Still, he had made her a simple appeal and she had brought it all on herself. She waited for him at half-past twelve on the appointed day.

Julia had said nothing to her aunt, who had company for luncheon and might mention his name – strange to go out with a man whose name you couldn't mention. He was late and she waited in the hall, listening to the echolalia of chatter from the luncheon party in the dining room. At one she answered the bell.

There in the outer hall stood a man whom she thought she had never seen before. His face was dead white and erratically shaven, his soft hat was crushed bun-like on his head, his shirt collar was dirty, and all except the band of his tie was out of sight. But at the moment when she recognised the figure as Dick Ragland she perceived a change which dwarfed the others into nothing; it was in his expression. His whole face was one prolonged sneer – the lids held with difficulty from covering the fixed eyes, the drooping mouth drawn up over the upper teeth, the chin wobbling like a made-over chin in which the paraffin had run – it was a face that both expressed and inspired disgust.

'H'lo,' he muttered.

For a minute she drew back from him; then, at a sudden silence from the dining room that gave on the hall, inspired by the silence in the hall itself, she half pushed him over the threshold, stepped out herself and closed the door behind them.

'Oh-h-h!' she said in a single, shocked breath.

'Haven't been home since yest'day. Got involve' on a party at –'

With repugnance, she turned him around by his arm and stumbled with him down the apartment stairs, passing the concierge's wife, who peered out at them curiously from her glass room. Then they came out into the bright sunshine of the rue Guynemer.

Against the spring freshness of the Luxembourg Gardens opposite, he was even more grotesque. He frightened her; she looked desperately up and down the street for a taxi, but one turning the corner of the rue de Vaugirard disregarded her signal.

'Where'll we go to lunch?' he asked.

'You're in no shape to go to lunch. Don't you realise? You've got to go home and sleep.'

'I'm all right. I get a drink I'll be fine.'

A passing cab slowed up at her gesture.

'You go home and go to sleep. You're not fit to go anywhere.'

As he focused his eyes on her, realising her suddenly as something fresh, something new and lovely, something alien to the smoky and turbulent world where he had spent his recent hours, a faint current of reason flowed through him. She saw his mouth twist with vague awe, saw him make a vague attempt to stand up straight. The taxi yawned.

'Maybe you're right. Very sorry.'

'What's your address?'

He gave it and then tumbled into a corner, his face still struggling towards reality. Julia closed the door.

When the cab had driven off, she hurried across the street and into the Luxembourg Gardens as if someone were after her.

2

Quite by accident, she answered when he telephoned at seven that night. His voice was strained and shaking:

'I suppose there's not much use apologising for this morning. I didn't know what I was doing, but that's no excuse. But if you could let me see you for a while somewhere tomorrow – just for a minute – I'd like the chance of telling you in person how terribly sorry –'

'I'm busy tomorrow.'

'Well, Friday then, or any day.'

'I'm sorry, I'm very busy this week.'

'You mean you don't ever want to see me again?'

'Mr Ragland, I hardly see the use of going any further with this. Really, that thing this morning was a little too much. I'm very sorry. I hope you feel better. Goodbye.'

She put him entirely out of her mind. She had not even associated his reputation with such a spectacle – a heavy drinker was someone who sat up late and drank champagne and maybe in the small hours rode home singing. This spectacle at high noon was something else again. Julia was through.

Meanwhile there were other men with whom she lunched at Ciro's and danced in the Bois. There was a reproachful letter from Phil Hoffman in America. She liked Phil better for having been so right about this. A fortnight passed and she would have forgotten Dick Ragland, had she not heard his name mentioned with scorn in several conversations. Evidently he had done such things before.

Then, a week before she was due to sail, she ran into him in the booking department of the White Star Line. He was as handsome – she could hardly believe her eyes. He leant with an elbow on the desk, his fine figure erect, his yellow gloves as stainless as his clear, shining eyes. His strong, gay personality had affected the clerk who served him with fascinated deference; the stenographers behind looked up for a minute and exchanged a glance. Then he saw Julia; she nodded, and with a quick, wincing change of expression he raised his hat.

They were together by the desk a long time and the silence was oppressive.

'Isn't this a nuisance?' she said.

'Yes,' he said jerkily, and then: 'You going by the *Olympic*?'

'Oh, yes.'

'I thought you might have changed.'

'Of course not,' she said coldly.

'I thought of changing; in fact, I was here to ask about it.'

'That's absurd.'

'You don't hate the sight of me? So it'll make you seasick when we pass each other on the deck?'

She smiled. He seized his advantage:

'I've improved somewhat since we last met.'

'Don't talk about that.'

'Well then, you have improved. You've got the loveliest costume on I ever saw.'

This was presumptuous, but she felt herself shimmering a little at the compliment.

'You wouldn't consider a cup of coffee with me at the café next door, just to recover from this ordeal?'

How weak of her to talk to him like this, to let him make advances. It was like being under the fascination of a snake.

'I'm afraid I can't.' Something terribly timid and vulnerable came into his face, twisting a little sinew in her heart. 'Well, all right,' she shocked herself by saying.

Sitting at the sidewalk table in the sunlight, there was nothing to remind of that awful day two weeks ago. Jekyll and Hyde. He was courteous, he was charming, he was amusing. He made her feel, oh, so attractive! He presumed on nothing.

'Have you stopped drinking?' she asked.

'Not till the fifth.'

'Oh!'

'Not until I said I'd stop. Then I'll stop.'

When Julia rose to go, she shook her head at his suggestion of a further meeting.

'I'll see you on the boat. After your twenty-eighth birthday.'

'All right; one more thing: it fits in with the high price of crime that I did something inexcusable to the one girl I've ever been in love with in my life.'

She saw him the first day on board, and then her heart sank into her shoes as she realised at last how much she wanted him. No matter what his past was, no matter what he had done. Which was not to say that she would ever let him know, but only that he moved her chemically more than anyone she had ever met, that all other men seemed pale beside him.

He was popular on the boat; she heard that he was giving a party on the night of his twenty-eighth birthday. Julia was not invited; when they met they spoke pleasantly, nothing more.

It was the day after the fifth that she found him stretched in his deckchair looking wan and white. There were wrinkles on his fine brow and around his eyes, and his hand, as he reached for a cup of bouillon, was trembling. He was still there in the late afternoon, visibly suffering, visibly miserable. After three times around, Julia was irresistibly impelled to speak to him:

'Has the new era begun?'

He made a feeble effort to rise, but she motioned him not to and sat on the next chair.

'You look tired.'

'I'm just a little nervous. This is the first day in five years that I haven't had a drink.'

'It'll be better soon.'

'I know,' he said grimly.

'Don't weaken.'

'I won't.'

'Can't I help you in any way? Would you like a bromide?'

'I can't stand bromides,' he said almost crossly. 'No, thanks, I mean.'

Julia stood up: 'I know you feel better alone. Things will be brighter tomorrow.'

'Don't go, if you can stand me.'

Julia sat down again.

'Sing me a song – can you sing?'

'What kind of song?'

'Something sad – some sort of blues.'

She sang him Libby Holman's 'This is how the story ends', in a low, soft voice.

'That's good. Now sing another. Or sing that again.'

'All right. If you like, I'll sing to you all afternoon.'

3

The second day in New York he called her on the phone. 'I've missed you so,' he said. 'Have you missed me?'

'I'm afraid I have,' she said reluctantly.

'Much?'

'I've missed you a lot. Are you better?'

'I'm all right now. I'm still a little nervous, but I'm starting work tomorrow. When can I see you?'

'When you want.'

'This evening then. And look – say that again.'

'What?'

'That you're afraid you have missed me.'

'I'm afraid that I have,' said Julia obediently.

'Missed me,' he added.

'I'm afraid I have missed you.'

'All right. It sounds like a song when you say it.'

'Goodbye, Dick.'

'Goodbye, Julia dear.'

She stayed in New York two months instead of the fortnight she had intended, because he would not let her go. Work took the place of drink in the daytime, but afterwards he must see Julia.

Sometimes she was jealous of his work when he telephoned that he was too tired to go out after the theatre. Lacking drink, nightlife was less than nothing to him – something quite spoilt and well lost. For Julia, who never drank, it was a stimulus in itself – the music and the parade of dresses and the handsome couple they made dancing together. At first they saw Phil Hoffman once in a while; Julia considered that he took the matter rather badly; then they didn't see him any more.

A few unpleasant incidents occurred. An old schoolmate, Esther Cary, came to her to ask if she knew of Dick Ragland's reputation. Instead of growing angry, Julia invited her to meet Dick and was delighted with the ease with which Esther's convictions were changed. There were other, small, annoying episodes, but Dick's misdemeanours had, fortunately, been confined to Paris and assumed here a far-away unreality. They loved each other deeply now – the memory of that morning slowly being effaced from Julia's imagination – but she wanted to be sure.

'After six months, if everything goes along like this, we'll announce our engagement. After another six months we'll be married.'

'Such a long time,' he mourned.

'But there were five years before that,' Julia answered. 'I trust you with my heart and with my mind, but something else says wait. Remember, I'm also deciding for my children.'

Those five years – oh, so lost and gone.

In August, Julia went to California for two months to see her family. She wanted to know how Dick would get along alone. They wrote every day; his letters were by turns cheerful, depressed, weary and hopeful. His work was going better. As things came back to him, his uncle had begun really to believe in him, but all the time he missed his Julia so. It was when an occasional note of despair began to appear that she cut her visit short by a week and came East to New York.

'Oh, thank God you're here!' he cried as they linked arms and walked out of the Grand Central station. 'It's been so hard. Half a dozen times lately I've wanted to go on a bust and I had to think of you, and you were so far away.'

'Darling – darling, you're so tired and pale. You're working too hard.'

'No, only that life is so bleak alone. When I go to bed my mind churns on and on. Can't we get married sooner?'

'I don't know; we'll see. You've got your Julia near you now, and nothing matters.'

After a week, Dick's depression lifted. When he was sad, Julia made him her baby, holding his handsome head against her breast, but she liked it best when he was confident and could cheer her up, making her laugh and feel taken care of and secure. She had rented an apartment with another girl and she took courses in biology and domestic science in Columbia. When deep fall came, they went to football games and the new shows together, and walked through the first snow in Central Park, and several times a week spent long evenings together in front of her fire. But time was going by and they were both impatient. Just before Christmas, an unfamiliar visitor – Phil Hoffman – presented himself at her door. It was the first time in many months. New York, with its quality of many independent ladders set side by side, is unkind to even the meetings of close friends; so, in the case of strained relations, meetings are easy to avoid.

And they were strange to each other. Since his expressed scepticism of Dick, he was automatically her enemy; on another count, she saw that he had improved, some of the hard angles were worn off; he was now an assistant district attorney, moving around with increasing confidence through his profession.

'So you're going to marry Dick?' he said. 'When?'

'Soon now. When Mother comes East.'

He shook his head emphatically. 'Julia, don't marry Dick. This isn't jealousy – I know when I am licked – but it seems awful for a lovely girl like you to take a blind dive into a lake full of rocks. What makes you think that people change their courses? Sometimes they dry up or even flow into a parallel channel, but I've never known anybody to change.'

'Dick's changed.'

'Maybe so. But isn't that an enormous "maybe"? If he was un-attractive and you liked him, I'd say go ahead with it. Maybe I'm all wrong, but it's so darn obvious that what fascinates you is that handsome pan of his and those attractive manners.'

'You don't know him,' Julia answered loyally. 'He's different with me. You don't know how gentle he is, and responsive. Aren't you being rather small and mean?'

'Hm.' Phil thought for a moment. 'I want to see you again in a few days. Or perhaps I'll speak to Dick.'

'You let Dick alone,' she cried. 'He has enough to worry him without your nagging him. If you were his friend you'd try to help him instead of coming to me behind his back.'

'I'm your friend first.'

'Dick and I are one person now.'

But three days later Dick came to see her at an hour when he would usually have been at the office.

'I'm here under compulsion,' he said lightly, 'under threat of exposure by Phil Hoffman.'

Her heart dropping like a plummet. 'Has he given up?' she thought. 'Is he drinking again?'

'It's about a girl. You introduced me to her last summer and told me to be very nice to her – Esther Cary.'

Now her heart was beating slowly.

'After you went to California I was lonesome and I ran into her. She'd liked me that day, and for a while we saw quite a bit of each other. Then you came back and I broke it off. It was a little difficult; I hadn't realised that she was so interested.'

'I see.' Her voice was starved and aghast.

'Try and understand. Those terribly lonely evenings. I think if it hadn't been for Esther, I'd have fallen off the wagon. I never loved her – I never loved anybody but you – but I had to see somebody who liked me.'

He put his arm around her, but she felt cold all over and he drew away.

'Then any woman would have done,' Julia said slowly. 'It didn't matter who.'

'No!' he cried.

'I stayed away so long to let you stand on your own feet and get back your self-respect by yourself.'

'I only love you, Julia.'

'But any woman can help you. So you don't really need me, do you?'

His face wore that vulnerable look that Julia had seen several times before; she sat on the arm of his chair and ran her hand over his cheek.

'Then what do you bring me?' she demanded. 'I thought that there'd be the accumulated strength of having beaten your weakness. What do you bring me now?'

'Everything I have.'

She shook her head. 'Nothing. Just your good looks – and the head waiter at dinner last night had that.'

They talked for two days and decided nothing. Sometimes she would pull him close and reach up to his lips that she loved so well, but her arms seemed to close around straw.

'I'll go away and give you a chance to think it over,' he said despairingly. 'I can't see any way of living without you, but I suppose you can't marry a man you don't trust or believe in. My uncle wanted me to go to London on some business –'

The night he left, it was sad on the dim pier. All that kept her from breaking was that it was not an image of strength that was leaving her; she would be just as strong without him. Yet as the murky lights fell on the fine structure of his brow and chin, as she saw the faces turn towards him, the eyes that followed him, an awful emptiness seized her and she wanted to say: 'Never mind, dear; we'll try it together.'

But try what? It was human to risk the toss between failure and success, but to risk the desperate gamble between adequacy and disaster –

'Oh, Dick, be good and be strong and come back to me. Change, change, Dick – change!'

'Goodbye Julia – goodbye.'

She last saw him on the deck, his profile cut sharp as a cameo against a match as he lit a cigarette.

4

It was Phil Hoffman who was to be with her at the beginning and at the end. It was he who broke the news as gently as it could be broken. He reached her apartment at half-past eight and carefully threw away the morning paper outside. Dick Ragland had disappeared at sea.

After her first wild burst of grief, he became purposely a little cruel.

'He knew himself. His will had given out; he didn't want life any more. And, Julia, just to show you how little you can possibly blame yourself, I'll tell you this: he'd hardly gone to his office for four months

– since you went to California. He wasn't fired because of his uncle; the business he went to London on was of no importance at all. After his first enthusiasm was gone he'd given up.'

She looked at him sharply. 'He didn't drink, did he? He wasn't drinking?'

For a fraction of a second Phil hesitated. 'No, he didn't drink; he kept his promise – he held on to that.'

'That was it,' she said. 'He kept his promise and he killed himself doing it.'

Phil waited uncomfortably.

'He did what he said he would and broke his heart doing it,' she went on chokingly. 'Oh, isn't life cruel sometimes – so cruel, never to let anybody off. He was so brave – he died doing what he said he'd do.'

Phil was glad he had thrown away the newspaper that hinted of Dick's gay evening in the bar – one of the many gay evenings that Phil had known of in the past few months. He was relieved that was over, because Dick's weakness had threatened the happiness of the girl he loved; but he was terribly sorry for him – even understanding how it was necessary for him to turn his maladjustment to life towards one mischief or another – but he was wise enough to leave Julia with the dream that she had saved out of wreckage.

There was a bad moment a year later, just before their marriage, when she said:

'You'll understand the feeling I have and always will have about Dick, won't you, Phil? It wasn't just his good looks. I believed in him – and I was right in a way. He broke rather than bent; he was a ruined man, but not a bad man. In my heart I knew when I first looked at him.'

Phil winced, but he said nothing. Perhaps there was more behind it than they knew. Better let it all alone in the depths of her heart and the depths of the sea.

What a Handsome Pair!

1

At four o'clock on a November afternoon in 1902, Teddy Van Beck got out of a hansom cab in front of a brownstone house on Murray Hill. He was a tall, round-shouldered young man with a beaked nose and soft brown eyes in a sensitive face. In his veins quarrelled the blood of colonial governors and celebrated robber barons; in him the synthesis had produced, for that time and place, something different and something new.

His cousin, Helen Van Beck, waited in the drawing room. Her eyes were red from weeping, but she was young enough for it not to detract from her glossy beauty – a beauty that had reached the point where it seemed to contain in itself the secret of its own growth, as if it would go on increasing for ever. She was nineteen and, contrary to the evidence, she was extremely happy.

Teddy put his arm around her and kissed her cheek, and found it changing into her ear as she turned her face away. He held her for a moment, his own enthusiasm chilling; then he said:

'You don't seem very glad to see me.'

Helen had a premonition that this was going to be one of the most memorable scenes of her life, and with unconscious cruelty she set about extracting from it its full dramatic value. She sat in a corner of the couch, facing an easy chair.

'Sit there,' she commanded, in what was then admired as a 'regal manner', and then, as Teddy straddled the piano stool: 'No, don't sit there. I can't talk to you if you're going to revolve around.'

'Sit on my lap,' he suggested.

'No.'

Playing a one-handed flourish on the piano, he said, 'I can listen better here.'

Helen gave up hopes of beginning on the sad and quiet note.

'This is a serious matter, Teddy. Don't think I've decided it without a lot of consideration. I've got to ask you – to ask you to release me from our understanding.'

'What?' Teddy's face paled with shock and dismay.

'I'll have to tell you from the beginning. I've realised for a long time that we have nothing in common. You're interested in your music, and I can't even play chopsticks.' Her voice was weary as if with suffering; her small teeth tugged at her lower lip.

'What of it?' he demanded, relieved. 'I'm musician enough for both. You wouldn't have to understand banking to marry a banker, would you?'

'This is different,' Helen answered. 'What would we do together? One important thing is that you don't like riding; you told me you were afraid of horses.'

'Of course I'm afraid of horses,' he said, and added reminiscently: 'They try to bite me.'

'It makes it so –'

'I've never met a horse – socially, that is – who didn't try to bite me. They used to do it when I put the bridle on; then, when I gave up putting the bridle on, they began reaching their heads around trying to get at my calves.'

The eyes of her father, who had given her a Shetland at three, glistened, cold and hard, from her own.

'You don't even like the people I like, let alone the horses,' she said.

'I can stand them. I've stood them all my life.'

'Well, it would be a silly way to start a marriage. I don't see any grounds for mutual – mutual –'

'Riding?'

'Oh, not that.' Helen hesitated, and then said in an unconvinced tone, 'Probably I'm not clever enough for you.'

'Don't talk such stuff!' He demanded some truth: 'Who's the man?'

It took her a moment to collect herself. She had always resented Teddy's tendency to treat women with less ceremony than was the custom of the day. Often he was an unfamiliar, almost frightening young man.

'There is someone,' she admitted. 'It's someone I've always known slightly, but about a month ago, when I went to Southampton, I was – thrown with him.'

'Thrown from a horse?'

'Please, Teddy,' she protested gravely. 'I'd been getting more unhappy about you and me, and whenever I was with him everything seemed all right.' A note of exaltation that she would not conceal came into Helen's voice. She rose and crossed the room, her straight, slim legs outlined by the shadows of her dress. 'We rode and swam and played tennis together – did the things we both liked to do.'

He stared into the vacant space she had created for him. 'Is that all that drew you to this fellow?'

'No, it was more than that. He was thrilling to me like nobody has ever been.' She laughed. 'I think what really started me thinking about it was one day we came in from riding and everybody said aloud what a nice pair we made.'

'Did you kiss him?'

She hesitated. 'Yes, once.'

He got up from the piano stool. 'I feel as if I had a cannonball in my stomach,' he exclaimed.

The butler announced Mr Stuart Oldhorne.

'Is he the man?' Teddy demanded tensely.

She was rather upset and confused. 'He should have come later. Would you rather go without meeting him?'

But Stuart Oldhorne, made confident by his new sense of proprietorship, had followed the butler.

The two men regarded each other with a curious impotence of expression; there can be no communication between men in that position, for their relation is indirect and consists in how much each of them has possessed or will possess of the woman in question, so that their emotions pass through her divided self as through a bad telephone connection.

Stuart Oldhorne sat beside Helen, his polite eyes never leaving Teddy. He had the same glowing physical power as she. He had been a star athlete at Yale and a rough-rider in Cuba, and was the best young horseman on Long Island. Women loved him not only for his points but for a real sweetness of temper.

'You've lived so much in Europe that I don't often see you,' he said to Teddy. Teddy didn't answer and Stuart Oldhorne turned to Helen: 'I'm early; I didn't realise –'

'You came at the right time,' said Teddy rather harshly. 'I stayed to pay you my congratulations.'

To Helen's alarm, he turned and ran his fingers over the keyboard. Then he began.

What he was playing, neither Helen nor Stuart knew, but Teddy always remembered. He put his mind in order with a short résumé of the history of music, beginning with some chords from the *Messiah* and ending with Debussy's *La plus que lent*, which had an evocative quality for him, because he had first heard it the day his brother died. Then, pausing for an instant, he began to play more thoughtfully, and the lovers on the sofa could feel that they were alone – that he had left them and had no more traffic with them – and Helen's discomfort lessened. But the flight, the elusiveness of the music, piqued her, gave her a feeling of annoyance. If Teddy had played the current sentimental song from *Ermine*, and had played it with feeling, she would have understood and been moved, but he was plunging her suddenly into a world of mature emotions, whither her nature neither could nor wished to follow.

She shook herself slightly and said to Stuart: 'Did you buy the horse?'

'Yes, and at a bargain… Do you know I love you?'

'I'm glad,' she whispered.

The piano stopped suddenly. Teddy closed it and swung slowly around: 'Did you like my congratulations?'

'Very much,' they said together.

'It was pretty good,' he admitted. 'That last was only based on a little counterpoint. You see, the idea of it was that you make such a handsome pair.'

He laughed unnaturally; Helen followed him out into the hall.

'Goodbye, Teddy,' she said. 'We're going to be good friends, aren't we?'

'Aren't we?' he repeated. He winked without smiling, and with a clicking, despairing sound of his mouth, went out quickly.

For a moment Helen tried vainly to apply a measure to the situation, wondering how she had come off with him, realising reluctantly that she had never for an instant held the situation in her hands. She had a dim realisation that Teddy was larger in scale; then the very largeness frightened her and, with relief and a warm tide of emotion, she hurried into the drawing room and the shelter of her lover's arms.

Their engagement ran through a halcyon summer. Stuart visited Helen's family at Tuxedo, and Helen visited his family in Wheatley Hills. Before breakfast, their horses' hooves sedately scattered the dew in sentimental glades, or curtained them with dust as they raced on dirt roads. They bought a tandem bicycle and pedalled all over Long Island – which Mrs Cassius Ruthven, a contemporary Cato[14], considered 'rather fast' for a couple not yet married. They were seldom at rest, but when they were, they reminded people of His Move on a Gibson pillow.[15]

Helen's taste for sport was advanced for her generation. She rode nearly as well as Stuart and gave him a decent game in tennis. He taught her some polo, and they were golf-crazy when it was still considered a comic game. They liked to feel fit and cool together. They thought of themselves as a team, and it was often remarked how well mated they were. A chorus of pleasant envy followed in the wake of their effortless glamour.

They talked.

'It seems a pity you've got to go to the office,' she would say. 'I wish you did something we could do together, like taming lions.'

'I've always thought that in a pinch I could make a living breeding and racing horses,' said Stuart.

'I know you could, you darling.'

In August he bought a Thomas automobile[16] and toured all the way to Chicago with three other men. It was an event of national interest and their pictures were in all the papers. Helen wanted to go, but it wouldn't have been proper, so they compromised by driving down Fifth Avenue on a sunny September morning, one with the fine day and the fashionable crowd, but distinguished by their unity, which made them each as strong as two.

'What do you suppose?' Helen demanded. 'Teddy sent me the oddest present – a cup rack.'

Stuart laughed. 'Obviously he means that all we'll ever do is win cups.'

'I thought it was rather a slam,' Helen ruminated. 'I saw that he was invited to everything, but he didn't answer a single invitation. Would you mind very much stopping by his apartment now? I haven't seen him for months and I don't like to leave anything unpleasant in the past.'

He wouldn't go in with her. 'I'll sit and answer questions about the auto from passers-by.'

The door was opened by a woman in a cleaning cap, and Helen heard the sound of Teddy's piano from the room beyond. The woman seemed reluctant to admit her.

'He said don't interrupt him, but I suppose if you're his cousin –'

Teddy welcomed her, obviously startled and somewhat upset, but in a minute he was himself again.

'I won't marry you,' he assured her. 'You've had your chance.'

'All right,' she laughed.

'How are you?' He threw a pillow at her. 'You're beautiful! Are you happy with this – this centaur? Does he beat you with his riding crop?' He peered at her closely. 'You look a little duller than when I knew you. I used to whip you up to a nervous excitement that bore a resemblance to intelligence.'

'I'm happy, Teddy. I hope you are.'

'Sure, I'm happy; I'm working. I've got MacDowell on the run and I'm going to have a shebang at Carnegie Hall next September.' His eyes became malicious. 'What did you think of my girl?'

'Your girl?'

'The girl who opened the door for you.'

'Oh, I thought it was a maid.' She flushed and was silent.

He laughed. 'Hey, Betty!' he called. 'You were mistaken for the maid!'

'And that's the fault of my cleaning on Sunday,' answered a voice from the next room.

Teddy lowered his voice. 'Do you like her?' he demanded.

'Teddy!' She teetered on the arm of the sofa, wondering whether she should leave at once.

'What would you think if I married her?' he asked confidentially.

'Teddy!' She was outraged; it had needed but a glance to place the woman as common. 'You're joking. She's older than you... You wouldn't be such a fool as to throw away your future that way.'

He didn't answer.

'Is she musical?' Helen demanded. 'Does she help you with your work?'

'She doesn't know a note. Neither did you, but I've got enough music in me for twenty wives.'

Visualising herself as one of them, Helen rose stiffly.

'All I can ask you is to think how your mother would have felt – and those who care for you… Goodbye, Teddy.'

He walked out the door with her and down the stairs.

'As a matter of fact, we've been married for two months,' he said casually. 'She was a waitress in a place where I used to eat.'

Helen felt that she should be angry and aloof, but tears of hurt vanity were springing to her eyes.

'And do you love her?'

'I like her; she's a good person and good for me. Love is something else. I loved you, Helen, and that's all dead in me for the present. Maybe it's coming out in my music. Some day I'll probably love other women – or maybe there'll never be anything but you. Goodbye, Helen.'

The declaration touched her. 'I hope you'll be happy, Teddy. Bring your wife to the wedding.'

He bowed non-committally. When she had gone, he returned thoughtfully to his apartment.

'That was the cousin that I was in love with,' he said.

'And was it?' Betty's face, Irish and placid, brightened with interest. 'She's a pretty thing.'

'She wouldn't have been as good for me as a nice peasant like you.'

'Always thinking of yourself, Teddy Van Beck.'

He laughed. 'Sure I am, but you love me, anyhow?'

'That's a big wur-red.'

'All right. I'll remember that when you come begging around for a kiss. If my grandfather knew I married a bogtrotter, he'd turn over in his grave. Now get out and let me finish my work.'

He sat at the piano, a pencil behind his ear. Already his face was resolved, composed, but his eyes grew more intense minute by minute, until there was a glaze in them, behind which they seemed to have joined his ears in counting and hearing. Presently there was no more indication in his face that anything had occurred to disturb the tranquillity of his Sunday morning.

Mrs Cassius Ruthven and a friend, veils flung back across their hats, sat in their auto on the edge of the field.

'A young woman playing polo in breeches.' Mrs Ruthven sighed. 'Amy Van Beck's daughter. I thought when Helen organised the Amazons she'd stop at divided skirts. But her husband apparently has no objections, for there he stands, egging her on. Of course, they always have liked the same things.'

'A pair of thoroughbreds, those two,' said the other woman complacently, meaning that she admitted them to be her equals. 'You'd never look at them and think that anything had gone wrong.'

She was referring to Stuart's mistake in the panic of 1907. His father had bequeathed him a precarious situation and Stuart had made an error of judgement. His honour was not questioned and his crowd stood by him loyally but his usefulness in Wall Street was over and his small fortune gone.

He stood in a group of men with whom he would presently play, noting things to tell Helen after the game – she wasn't turning with the play soon enough and several times she was unnecessarily ridden off at important moments. Her ponies were sluggish – the penalty for playing with borrowed mounts – but she was, nevertheless, the best player on the field, and in the last minute she made a save that brought applause.

'Good girl! Good girl!'

Stuart had been delegated with the unpleasant duty of chasing the women from the field. They had started an hour late and now a team from New Jersey was waiting to play; he sensed trouble as he cut across to join Helen and walked beside her towards the stables. She was splendid, with her flushed cheeks, her shining, triumphant eyes, her short, excited breath. He temporised for a minute.

'That was good – at last,' he said.

'Thanks. It almost broke my arm. Wasn't I pretty good all through?'

'You were the best out there.'

'I know it.'

He waited while she dismounted and handed the pony to a groom.

'Helen, I believe I've got a job.'

'What is it?'

'Don't jump on the idea till you think it over. Gus Myers wants me to manage his racing stables. Eight thousand a year.'

Helen considered. 'It's a nice salary; and I bet you could make yourself up a nice string from his ponies.'

'The principal thing is that I need the money; I'd have as much as you and things would be easier.'

'You'd have as much as me,' Helen repeated. She almost regretted that he would need no more help from her. 'But with Gus Myers, isn't there a string attached? Wouldn't he expect a boost up?'

'He probably would,' answered Stuart bluntly, 'and if I can help him socially, I will. As a matter of fact, he wants me at a stag dinner tonight.'

'All right, then,' Helen said absently. Still hesitating to tell her her game was over, Stuart followed her glance towards the field, where a runabout had driven up and parked by the ropes.

'There's your old friend, Teddy,' he remarked dryly – 'or rather, your new friend, Teddy. He's taking a sudden interest in polo. Perhaps he thinks the horses aren't biting this summer.'

'You're not in a very good humour,' protested Helen. 'You know, if you say the word, I'll never see him again. All I want in the world is for you and I to be together.'

'I know,' he admitted regretfully. 'Selling horses and giving up clubs put a crimp in that. I know the women all fall for Teddy, now he's getting famous, but if he tries to fool around with you I'll break his piano over his head... Oh, another thing,' he began, seeing the men already riding on the field. 'About your last chukka –'

As best as he could, he put the situation up to her. He was not prepared for the fury that swept over her.

'But it's an outrage! I got up the game and it's been posted on the bulletin board for three days.'

'You started an hour late.'

'And do you know why?' she demanded. 'Because your friend Joe Morgan insisted that Celie ride side-saddle. He tore her habit off her three times, and she only got here by climbing out the kitchen window.'

'I can't do anything about it.'

'Why can't you? Weren't you once a governor of this club? How can women expect to be any good if they have to quit every time the men want the field? All the men want is for the women to come up to them in the evening and tell them what a beautiful game they played!'

Still raging and blaming Stuart, she crossed the field to Teddy's car. He got out and greeted her with concentrated intensity:

'I've reached the point where I can neither sleep nor eat from thinking of you. What point is that?'

There was something thrilling about him that she had never been conscious of in the old days; perhaps the stories of his philanderings had made him more romantic to her.

'Well, don't think of me as I am now,' she said. 'My face is getting rougher every day and my muscles lean out of an evening dress like a female impersonator. People are beginning to refer to me as handsome instead of pretty. Besides, I'm in a vile humour. It seems to me women are always just edged out of everything.'

Stuart's game was brutal that afternoon. In the first five minutes, he realised Teddy's runabout was no longer there, and his long slugs began to tally from all angles. Afterwards, he bumped home across country at a gallop; his mood was not assuaged by a note handed him by the children's nurse:

Dear: Since your friends made it impossible for us to play, I wasn't going to sit there dripping; so I had Teddy bring me home. And since you'll be out to dinner, I'm going into New York with him to the theatre. I'll either be out on the theatre train or spend the night at Mother's.

HELEN

Stuart went upstairs and changed into his dinner coat. He had no defence against the unfamiliar claws of jealousy that began a slow dissection of his insides. Often Helen had gone to plays or dances with other men, but this was different. He felt towards Teddy the faint contempt of the physical man for the artist, but the last six months had bruised his pride. He perceived the possibility that Helen might be seriously interested in someone else.

He was in a bad humour at Gus Myers' dinner – annoyed with his host for talking so freely about their business arrangement. When at last they rose from the table, he decided that it was no go and called Myers aside.

'Look here. I'm afraid this isn't a good idea, after all.'

'Why not?' His host looked at him in alarm. 'Are you going back on me? My dear fellow –'

'I think we'd better call it off.'

'And why, may I ask? Certainly I have the right to ask why.'

Stuart considered. 'All right, I'll tell you. When you made that little speech, you mentioned me as if you had somehow bought me, as if I were a sort of employee in your office. Now, in the sporting world that doesn't go; things are more – more democratic. I grew up with all these men here tonight, and they didn't like it any better than I did.'

'I see,' Mr Myers reflected carefully – 'I see.' Suddenly he clapped Stuart on the back. 'That is exactly the sort of thing I like to be told; it helps me. From now on I won't mention you as if you were in my – as if we had a business arrangement. Is that all right?'

After all, the salary was eight thousand dollars.

'Very well, then,' Stuart agreed. 'But you'll have to excuse me tonight. I'm catching a train to the city.'

'I'll put an automobile at your disposal.'

At ten o'clock he rang the bell of Teddy's apartment on Forty-eighth Street.

'I'm looking for Mr Van Beck,' he said to the woman who answered the door. 'I know he's gone to the theatre, but I wonder if you can tell me –' Suddenly he guessed who the woman was. 'I'm Stuart Oldhorne,' he explained. 'I married Mr Van Beck's cousin.'

'Oh, come in,' said Betty pleasantly. 'I know all about who you are.'

She was just this side of forty, stoutish and plain of face, but full of a keen, brisk vitality. In the living room they sat down.

'You want to see Teddy?'

'He's with my wife and I want to join them after the theatre. I wonder if you know where they went?'

'Oh, so Teddy's with your wife.' There was a faint, pleasant brogue in her voice. 'Well, now, he didn't say exactly where he'd be tonight.'

'Then you don't know?'

'I don't – not for the life of me,' she admitted cheerfully. 'I'm sorry.'

He stood up, and Betty saw the thinly hidden anguish in his face. Suddenly she was really sorry.

'I did hear him say something about the theatre,' she said ruminatively. 'Now sit down and let me think what it was. He goes out so much and a play once a week is enough for me, so that one night mixes up with the others in my head. Didn't your wife say where to meet them?'

'No. I only decided to come in after they'd started. She said she'd catch the theatre train back to Long Island or go to her Mother's.'

'That's it,' Betty said triumphantly, striking her hands together like cymbals. 'That's what he said when he called up – that he was putting a lady on the theatre train for Long Island, and would be home himself right afterwards. We've had a child sick and it's driven things from my mind.'

'I'm very sorry I bothered you under those conditions.'

'It's no bother. Sit down. It's only after ten.'

Feeling no easier, Stuart relaxed a little and accepted a cigar.

'No, if I tried to keep up with Teddy, I'd have white hair by now,' Betty said. 'Of course, I go to his concerts, but often I fall asleep – not that he ever knows it. So long as he doesn't take too much to drink and knows where his home is, I don't bother about where he wanders.' As Stuart's face grew serious again, she changed her tone: 'All in all, he's a good husband to me and we have a happy life together, without interfering with each other. How would he do working next to the nursery and groaning at every sound? And how would I do going to Mrs Ruthven's with him, and all of them talking about high society and high art?'

A phrase of Helen's came back to Stuart: 'Always together – I like for us to do everything together.'

'You have children, haven't you, Mr Oldhorne?'

'Yes. My boy's almost big enough to sit on a horse.'

'Ah, yes; you're both great for horses.'

'My wife says that as soon as their legs are long enough to reach stirrups, she'll be interested in them again.' This didn't sound right to Stuart and he modified it: 'I mean she always has been interested in

124

them, but she never let them monopolise her or come between us. We've always believed that marriage ought to be founded on companionship, on having the same interests. I mean, you're musical and you help your husband.'

Betty laughed. 'I wish Teddy could hear that. I can't read a note or carry a tune.'

'No?' He was confused. 'I'd somehow got the impression that you were musical.'

'You can't see why else he'd have married me?'

'Not at all. On the contrary.'

After a few minutes, he said goodnight, somehow liking her. When he had gone, Betty's expression changed slowly to one of exasperation; she went to the telephone and called her husband's studio:

'There you are, Teddy. Now listen to me carefully. I know your cousin is with you and I want to talk with her... Now, don't lie. You put her on the phone. Her husband has been here, and if you don't let me talk to her, it might be a serious matter.'

She could hear an unintelligible colloquy, and then Helen's voice: 'Hello.'

'Good evening, Mrs Oldhorne. Your husband came here, looking for you and Teddy. I told him I didn't know which play you were at, so you'd better be thinking which one. And I told him Teddy was leaving you at the station in time for the theatre train.'

'Oh, thank you very much. We –'

'Now, you meet your husband or there's trouble for you, or I'm no judge of men. And – wait a minute. Tell Teddy, if he's going to be up late, that Josie's sleeping light, and he's not to touch the piano when he gets home.'

Betty heard Teddy come in at eleven, and she came into the drawing room smelling of camomile vapour. He greeted her absently; there was a look of suffering in his face and his eyes were bright and far away.

'You call yourself a great musician, Teddy Van Beck,' she said, 'but it seems to me you're much more interested in women.'

'Let me alone, Betty.'

'I do let you alone, but when the husbands start coming here, it's another matter.'

'This was different, Betty. This goes way back into the past.'

'It sounds like the present to me.'

'Don't make any mistake about Helen,' he said. 'She's a good woman.'

'Not through any fault of yours, I know.'

He sank his head wearily in his hands. 'I've tried to forget her. I've avoided her for six years. And then, when I met her a month ago, it all rushed over me. Try and understand, Bet. You're my best friend; you're the only person that ever loved me.'

'When you're good I love you,' she said.

'Don't worry. It's over. She loves her husband; she just came to New York with me because she's got some spite against him. She follows me a certain distance just like she always has, and then – Anyhow, I'm not going to see her any more. Now go to bed, Bet. I want to play for a while.'

He was on his feet when she stopped him.

'You're not to touch the piano tonight.'

'Oh, I forgot about Josie,' he said remorsefully. 'Well, I'll drink a bottle of beer and then I'll come to bed.'

He came close and put his arm around her.

'Dear Bet, nothing could ever interfere with us.'

'You're a bad boy, Teddy,' she said. 'I wouldn't ever be so bad to you.'

'How do you know, Bet? How do you know what you'd do?'

He smoothed down her plain brown hair, knowing for the thousandth time that she had none of the world's dark magic for him, and that he couldn't live without her for six consecutive hours. 'Dear Bet,' he whispered. 'Dear Bet.'

3

The Oldhornes were visiting. In the last four years, since Stuart had terminated his bondage to Gus Myers, they had become visiting people. The children visited Grandmother Van Beck during the winter and attended school in New York. Stuart and Helen visited friends in Asheville, Aiken and Palm Beach, and in the summer usually occupied a small cottage on someone's Long Island estate. 'My dear, it's just standing there empty. I wouldn't dream of accepting any rent. You'll be doing us a favour by occupying it.'

Usually, they were; they gave out a great deal of themselves in that eternal willingness and enthusiasm which makes a successful guest – it became their profession. Moving through a world that was growing rich with the war in Europe, Stuart had somewhere lost his way. Twice playing brilliant golf in the national amateur, he accepted a job as professional at a club which his father had helped to found. He was restless and unhappy.

This weekend they were visiting a pupil of his. As a consequence of a mixed foursome, the Oldhornes went upstairs to dress for dinner surcharged with the unpleasant accumulation of many unsatisfactory months. In the afternoon, Stuart had played with their hostess and Helen with another man – a situation which Stuart always dreaded, because it forced him into competition with Helen. He had actually tried to miss that putt on the eighteenth – to just miss it. But the ball dropped in the cup. Helen went through the superficial motions of a good loser, but she devoted herself pointedly to her partner for the rest of the afternoon.

These expressions still counterfeited amusement as they entered their room.

When the door closed, Helen's pleasant expression faded and she walked towards the dressing table as though her own reflection was the only decent company with which to foregather. Stuart watched her, frowning.

'I know why you're in a rotten humour,' he said; 'though I don't believe you know yourself.'

'I'm not in a rotten humour,' Helen responded in a clipped voice.

'You are; and I know the real reason – the one you don't know. It's because I holed that putt this afternoon.'

She turned slowly, incredulously, from the mirror.

'Oh, so I have a new fault! I've suddenly become, of all things, a poor sport!'

'It's not like you to be a poor sport,' he admitted, 'but otherwise why all this interest in other men, and why do you look at me as if I'm – well, slightly gamy?'

'I'm not aware of it.'

'I am.' He was aware, too, that there was always some man in their life now – some man of power and money who paid court to Helen and gave her the sense of solidity which he failed to provide. He had no cause to be jealous of any particular man, but the pressure of many was irritating. It annoyed him that on so slight a grievance, Helen should remind him by her actions that he no longer filled her entire life.

'If Anne can get any satisfaction out of winning, she's welcome to it,' said Helen suddenly.

'Isn't that rather petty? She isn't in your class; she won't qualify for the third flight in Boston.'

Feeling herself in the wrong, she changed her tone.

'Oh, that isn't it,' she broke out. 'I just keep wishing you and I could play together like we used to. And now you have to play with dubs, and get their wretched shots out of traps. Especially' – she hesitated – 'especially when you're so unnecessarily gallant.'

The faint contempt in her voice, the mock jealousy that covered a growing indifference was apparent to him. There had been a time when, if he danced with another woman, Helen's stricken eyes followed him around the room.

'My gallantry is simply a matter of business,' he answered. 'Lessons have brought in three hundred a month all summer. How could I go to see you play at Boston next week, except that I'm going to coach other women?'

'And you're going to see me win,' announced Helen. 'Do you know that?'

'Naturally, I want nothing more,' Stuart said automatically. But the unnecessary defiance in her voice repelled him, and he suddenly wondered if he really cared whether she won or not.

At the same moment, Helen's mood changed and for a moment she saw the true situation – that she could play in amateur tournaments and Stuart could not, that the new cups in the rack were all hers now, that he had given up the fiercely competitive sportsmanship that had been the breath of life to him in order to provide necessary money.

'Oh, I'm so sorry for you, Stuart!' There were tears in her eyes. 'It seems such a shame that you can't do the things you love, and I can. Perhaps I oughtn't to play this summer.'

'Nonsense,' he said. 'You can't sit at home and twirl your thumbs.'

She caught at this: 'You wouldn't want me to. I can't help being good at sports; you taught me nearly all I know. But I wish I could help you.'

'Just try to remember I'm your best friend. Sometimes you act as if we were rivals.'

She hesitated, annoyed by the truth of his words and unwilling to concede an inch; but a wave of memories rushed over her, and she thought how brave he was in his eked-out, pieced-together life; she came and threw her arms around him.

'Darling, darling, things are going to be better. You'll see.'

Helen won the finals in the tournament at Boston the following week. Following around with the crowd, Stuart was very proud of her. He hoped that instead of feeding her egotism, the actual achievement would make things easier between them. He hated the conflict that had grown out of their wanting the same excellences, the same prizes from life.

Afterwards he pursued her progress towards the clubhouse, amused and a little jealous of the pack that fawned around her. He reached the club among the last, and a steward accosted him. 'Professionals are served in the lower grill, please,' the man said.

'That's all right. My name's Oldhorne.'

He started to walk by, but the man barred his way.

'Sorry, sir. I realise that Mrs Oldhorne's playing in the match, but my orders are to direct the professionals to the lower grill, and I understand you are a professional.'

'Why, look here –' Stuart began, wildly angry, and stopped. A group of people were listening. 'All right; never mind,' he said gruffly, and turned away.

The memory of the experience rankled; it was the determining factor that drove him, some weeks later, to a momentous decision. For a long time he had been playing with the idea of joining the Canadian Air Force, for service in France. He knew that his absence would have little practical bearing on the lives of Helen and the children; happening on some friends who were also full of the restlessness of 1915, the matter was suddenly decided. But he had not counted on the effect upon Helen; her reaction was not so much one of grief or alarm, but as if she had been somehow outwitted.

'But you might have told me!' she wailed. 'You leave me dangling; you simply take yourself away without any warning.'

Once again Helen saw him as the bright and intolerably blinding hero, and her soul winced before him as it had when they first met. He was a warrior; for him, peace was only the interval between wars, and peace was destroying him. Here was the game of games beckoning him – without throwing over the whole logic of their lives, there was nothing she could say.

'This is my sort of thing,' he said confidently, younger with his excitement. 'A few more years of this life and I'd go to pieces, take to drink. I've somehow lost your respect, and I've got to have that, even if I'm far away.'

She was proud of him again; she talked to everyone of his impending departure. Then, one September afternoon, she came home from the city, full of the old feeling of comradeship and bursting with news, to find him buried in an utter depression.

'Stuart,' she cried, 'I've got the –' She broke off. 'What's the matter, darling? Is something the matter?'

He looked at her dully. 'They turned me down,' he said.

'What?'

'My left eye.' He laughed bitterly. 'Where that dub cracked me with the brassie. I'm nearly blind in it.'

'Isn't there anything you can do?'

'Nothing.'

'Stuart!' She stared at him aghast. 'Stuart, and I was going to tell you! I was saving it for a surprise. Elsa Prentice has organised a Red Cross unit to serve with the French, and I joined it because I thought it would be wonderful if we both went. We've been measured for uniforms and bought our outfits, and we're sailing the end of next week.'

4

Helen was a blurred figure among other blurred figures on a boat deck, dark against the threat of submarines. When the ship had slid out into the obscure future, Stuart walked eastward along Fifty-seventh Street. His grief at the severance of many ties was a weight he carried in his body, and he walked slowly, as if adjusting himself to it. To balance this there was a curious sensation of lightness in his mind. For the first time in twelve years he was alone, and the feeling came over him that he was alone for good; knowing Helen and knowing war, he could guess at the experiences she would go through, and he could not form any picture of a renewed life together afterwards. He was discarded; she had proved the stronger at last. It seemed very strange and sad that his marriage should have such an ending.

He came to the Carnegie Hall, dark after a concert, and his eye caught the name of Theodore Van Beck, large on the posted bills. As he stared at it, a green door opened in the side of the building and a group of people in evening dress came out. Stuart and Teddy were face to face before they recognised each other.

'Hello, there!' Teddy cried cordially. 'Did Helen sail?'

'Just now.'

'I met her on the street yesterday and she told me. I wanted you both to come to my concert. Well, she's quite a heroine, going off like that... Have you met my wife?'

Stuart and Betty smiled at each other.

'We've met.'

'And I didn't know it,' protested Teddy. 'Women need watching when they get towards their dotage... Look here, Stuart; we're having a few people up to the apartment. No heavy music or anything. Just supper and a few debutantes to tell me I was divine. It will do you good to come. I imagine you're missing Helen like the devil.'

'I don't think I –'

'Come along. They'll tell you you're divine too.'

Realising that the invitation was inspired by kindliness, Stuart accepted. It was the sort of gathering he had seldom attended, and he was surprised to meet so many people he knew. Teddy played the lion in a manner at once assertive and sceptical. Stuart listened as he enlarged to Mrs Cassius Ruthven on one of his favourite themes:

'People tried to make marriages cooperative and they've ended by becoming competitive. Impossible situation. Smart men will get to fight shy of ornamental women. A man ought to marry somebody who'll be grateful, like Betty here.'

'Now don't talk so much, Theodore Van Beck,' Betty interrupted. 'Since you're such a fine musician, you'd do well to express yourself with music instead of rash words.'

'I don't agree with your husband,' said Mrs Ruthven. 'English girls hunt with their men and play politics with them on absolutely equal terms, and it tends to draw them together.'

'It does not,' insisted Teddy. 'That's why English society is the most disorganised in the world. Betty and I are happy because we haven't any qualities in common at all.'

His exuberance grated on Stuart, and the success that flowed from him swung his mind back to the failure of his own life. He could not know that his life was not destined to be a failure. He could not read the fine story that three years later would be carved proud above his soldier's grave, or know that his restless body, which never spared itself in sport or danger, was destined to give him one last proud gallop at the end.

'They turned me down,' he was saying to Mrs Ruthven. 'I'll have to stick to Squadron A, unless we get drawn in.'

'So Helen's gone.' Mrs Ruthven looked at him, reminiscing. 'I'll never forget your wedding. You were both so handsome, so ideally suited to each other. Everybody spoke of it.'

Stuart remembered; for the moment it seemed that he had little else that it was fun to remember.

'Yes,' he agreed, nodding his head thoughtfully, 'I suppose we were a handsome pair.'

Notes

1. A member of Skull and Bones, a mysterious Yale-based secret society with a powerful alumni network.

2. Nathan Hale, a martyr soldier of the American Revolution, who was hanged as a spy in New York on 22nd September 1776.

3. The Almanach de Gotha was published continuously from 1763–1944. It charted royal genealogies.

4. Gian Lorenzo Bernini (1598–1680), Italian painter, sculptor and architect.

5. Provisional government formed in 1917. It was dissolved by the Bolsheviks later in the same year, and Chairman Alexander Kerensky fled abroad.

6. Anton Ivanovich Denikin (1872–1947) commanded an anti-Bolshevik army. He gained control of a large part of South Russia, but failed to capture Moscow. Driven back by the soviet forces, his army was demoralised. He resigned his command, fled to France and eventually died in America.

7. Many North Americans were increasingly concerned about the morality of slavery in 1858, although it was not declared illegal until 1865.

8. Sites of battles of the Civil War.

9. Thomas Henry Huxley (1825–95), physiologist, anatomist, anthropologist, agnostic and educator; Herbert Spencer (1820–1903), British philosopher and sociologist.

10. *The Saturday Evening Post* printed this as 'lobster American was really lobster American', which obviously makes no sense. Lobster with 'sauce à l'américaine' was invented in 1867 by chef Noel Peters, but some French restaurateurs disliked this name and instead called it 'sauce à l'armoricaine' from the old name for Brittany, l'Armorique.

11. 'Oh, this is terrible! Is there nothing that can be done?'

12. Alain Gerbault (1893–1941), one of France's greatest single-handed sailors. He crossed the Atlantic in 1923 and circumnavigated the world during 1925–29. He died in the South Seas in 1941.

13. A quotation from 'Stanzas Written in Dejection Near Naples' by Percy Bysshe Shelley (1792–1822). The third line should run 'Around its unexpanded buds'.

14. Cato the Elder (234–149 BC), a Roman politician also known as Cato the Censor, was renowned for his devotion to the traditional Roman way of life, and criticisms of extravagance and new customs. His disapproval of Carthage was partly responsible for the Third Punic War.

15. Charles Dana Gibson (1867-1944), famous illustrator and creator of the 'Gibson Girl', had his work reproduced and merchandised in a wide variety of media, including pillow covers. The print 'The Greatest Game in the World: His Move' depicts a young couple enraptured in each other to the extent of ignoring the chess game they are playing. The publisher wishes to acknowledge the help of Chris Sheppard and Richard Davies in uncovering the reference.

16. An American one-cylinder automobile, first manufactured in 1899. A modified model won the 1908 New York to Paris (Round-the-World) Race.

Biographical note

Francis Scott Key Fitzgerald was born in 1896 in St Paul, Minnesota. His parents were middle class, but not particularly wealthy, and had to save to put Fitzgerald through private school and Princeton University. Ambitious to become a writer, Fitzgerald neglected his studies, was put on academic probation, and in 1917 left Princeton to join the army. Shortly before his posting, he submitted his first manuscript, 'The Romantic Egotist', to Scribners; it was rejected, but with a letter encouraging him to rework and resubmit the story.

In 1918, Fitgerald was posted to Camp Sheridan in Alabama. He was never sent abroad to active service, but during his time in the South, he met and fell in love with Zelda Sayre, the eighteen-year-old daughter of a local judge. They became engaged, and when Fitzgerald's manuscript – now titled *This Side of Paradise* – was finally accepted by Scribners in 1919, they married. The novel dealt with the boredom and disillusionment of the social elite at Princeton after the war, and brought Fitzgerald immediate acclaim. The Fitzgeralds embarked on a life of social excess in New York, and though a number of short stories and a second novel, *The Beautiful and the Damned* (1922), followed in the next two years, Fitzgerald's critical image was compromised by their extravagant lifestyle.

The Fitzgeralds moved back to Minnesota for the birth of their daughter Frances Scott Fitzgerald in 1921, but the social life of New York remained a distraction and hampered Fitzgerald's attempts at writing. Finally in 1924, the family moved to France, seeking a more subdued atmosphere, and here, in Valescure on the Côte d'Azur, Fitzgerald wrote *The Great Gatsby*. This novel, widely considered his masterpiece, deals with his perennial themes of money, class, and jazz-age social degeneration, and has been hailed as a candidate for the 'great American novel'.

The Fitzgeralds remained in France for the next three years, alternating between the Riviera and Paris, where Fitzgerald met the then little-known Ernest Hemingway, but the atmosphere of France proved unconducive both to Fitzgerald's writing and to Zelda's mental health. After a brief return to America, Zelda suffered her first breakdown in 1930 and was moved to a Swiss clinic for treatment, which Fitzgerald financed with the proceeds of new short stories.

His fourth novel was finally finished in 1934. *Tender is the Night* was the story of a psychologist and his damaging marriage to a schizophrenic and reflected his unease with his own marriage to Zelda, who was now frequently in and out of mental institutions and had penned her own autobiographical novel, *Save Me the Waltz*, in 1932. The new novel was not a commercial success and, by the mid-1930s, Fitzgerald was in serious financial difficulty. After a period spent in hotels in North Carolina, where Zelda was in Highland Hospital, he moved to Hollywood to work on film adaptations and screenplays. His final novel, *The Last Tycoon*, was inspired by his experiences in Hollywood, but was left unfinished when he died of a heart attack in 1940.

HESPERUS PRESS

Hesperus Press, as suggested by the Latin motto, is committed to bringing near what is far – far both in space and time. Works written by the greatest authors, and unjustly neglected or simply little known in the English-speaking world, are made accessible through new translations and a completely fresh editorial approach. Through these classic works, the reader is introduced to the greatest writers from all times and all cultures.

For more information on Hesperus Press, please visit our website: **www.hesperuspress.com**

ET REMOTISSIMA PROPE

MODERN VOICES

SELECTED TITLES FROM HESPERUS PRESS

Author	Title	Foreword writer
Mikhail Bulgakov	*A Dog's Heart*	A.S. Byatt
Mikhail Bulgakov	*The Fatal Eggs*	Doris Lessing
F. Scott Fitzgerald	*The Rich Boy*	John Updike
Franz Kafka	*Metamorphosis*	Martin Jarvis
Franz Kafka	*The Trial*	Zadie Smith
Carlo Levi	*Words are Stones*	Anita Desai
André Malraux	*The Way of the Kings*	Rachel Seiffert
Katherine Mansfield	*In a German Pension*	Linda Grant
Katherine Mansfield	*Prelude*	William Boyd
Vladimir Mayakovsky	*My Discovery of America*	Colum McCann
Luigi Pirandello	*Loveless Love*	
Jean-Paul Sartre	*The Wall*	Justin Cartwright